Ho ... oller
wa ...

A scream ripped from her throat. "My children! Someone's taken my children!"

She ran outside and saw a man pushing the stroller across the lot. "Stop! Give me my children!" At breakneck speed she ran after him, unaware that Cole was running beside her.

Her agonized cry sliced through him, and he willed his legs to move faster. Seconds later his stomach clenched as he saw the abductor shove the stroller toward the street. Holly let out a loud scream as the twins rolled into the path of an oncoming car.

With only seconds to react, Cole raced toward the stroller. Loud wails erupted from the children as he grasped the handle. But it was too late. He shoved the stroller away just as the car hit him. Breath left his body as he was thrown into the air. The last he remembered was the sound of Holly screaming his name.

Sandra Robbins is an award-winning, multipublished author of Christian fiction who lives with her husband in Tennessee. Without the support of her wonderful husband, four children and five grandchildren, it would be impossible for her to write. It is her prayer that God will use her words to plant seeds of hope in the lives of her readers so they may come to know the peace she draws from her life.

Books by Sandra Robbins

Love Inspired Suspense

Guarding the Babies

Smoky Mountain Secrets

In a Killer's Sights
Stalking Season
Ranch Hideout
Point Blank

Bounty Hunters

Fugitive Trackdown
Fugitive at Large
Yuletide Fugitive Threat

The Cold Case Files

Dangerous Waters
Yuletide Jeopardy
Trail of Secrets

Visit the Author Profile page at Harlequin.com for more titles.

GUARDING THE BABIES

SANDRA ROBBINS

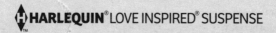

Recycling programs
for this product may
not exist in your area.

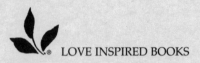 LOVE INSPIRED BOOKS

ISBN-13: 978-1-335-49023-0

Guarding the Babies

Copyright © 2018 by Sandra Robbins

www.Harlequin.com

Printed in U.S.A.

Keep thy heart with all diligence;
for out of it are the issues of life.
—Proverbs 4:23

To my own twins, Scott and Stacey,
who've brought me so much joy

ONE

Something wasn't right. Holly knew it the moment she opened her eyes. She lay still and squinted into the darkness that covered the bedroom. A puzzled frown pulled at her forehead. What had woken her?

Outside, the wind stirred and a branch on the oak tree next to her bedroom window tapped on the glass pane. In the distance, she could hear a dog barking, but there were no other sounds in the night to alarm her.

Then it hit her, and she bolted up in bed. It wasn't the presence of sounds that had awakened her. It was the *absence* of them. She reached over and switched on the bedside light and peered at the baby monitor on the table.

Silence greeted her.

How could that be? She'd left the quiet music playing in the nursery when she'd put her one-year-old niece and nephew to bed, as it seemed to lull them to sleep. Now there was nothing coming over the monitor. Not even the quiet snuffling sound that Emma often made in her sleep.

She flicked the covers back and bounded out of

bed. Without waiting to put on her robe or shoes, she ran down the hallway to the bedroom where Emma and Ethan slept. Her heart dropped to the pit of her stomach when she caught sight of the closed door that she had left open before she'd retired to her own room.

Fighting back the rising fear that threatened to overcome her, she threw the door open and switched on the overhead light. She didn't know what she expected to find, but it wasn't the sight of a figure dressed in black with a ski mask over his face, holding Ethan, and he was about to slip Ethan into the canvas baby carrier that lay against his chest. For a moment, all she could do was stare in shock. Then she went into full panic mode.

"What are you doing?" she screamed.

The man whirled around and dropped Ethan back in his bed. The room that moments ago had been sheathed in silence erupted with the startled cries of the awakened twins and a muttered exclamation of surprise from the intruder. He glared at her through the slits in his mask, and she cast a terrified glance from him to the two babies, who by now were standing in their cribs with their hands locked on the railings. Their alarmed cries echoed through the room.

Before she could move, the man lunged toward her, and she reacted on instinct. She darted to the rocking chair that sat to her left and positioned herself behind it. A soft chuckle drifted to her ears. "That ain't gonna protect you, lady."

He took another step in her direction, and she backed away toward the wall. As her foot touched the baseboard, she felt something nudge her back and remembered the broom she'd left there earlier.

She wrapped both hands around the broom's handle and held it in front of her like a sword, poised to strike her attacker. He shook his head, and his lips visible through the mask's mouth opening curled into a sarcastic smile. "A broom?" he taunted. "That the best you can do?"

Holly willed herself not to move until he'd taken another step closer, and then she reacted. With a fierce growl, she thrust the head of the broom forward and jabbed at the mask's eye slits. The man howled in pain as the sharp bristles connected with his eyes, and he staggered backward and clutched at his face. Before he could retreat farther, she readjusted her hands on the broom and swung with all her might. The blow hit him on the side of the head.

He stumbled but caught himself and snarled, "You're going to pay for that."

"I don't think so!" she yelled.

Before he could take another step, she drew back, and with the full weight of her body, she slammed the end of the handle into his abdomen. She didn't give him time to collect his wits before she took a deep breath and delivered a hard thrust to his Adam's apple.

A gurgling sound erupted from his throat, and he grabbed at his neck in obvious pain as he backed away. His chest heaved as he tried to breathe, but she didn't give up. She advanced on him, continuously jabbing and thrusting the broom, as he turned to run from the room. "Get out of my house!" she screamed with each step she took.

He tried to flee from the blows, but it was no use.

She was a mama bear protecting her young, and she wasn't about to let this man who'd sneaked into her house in the middle of the night hurt her or her family.

As he stumbled into the hallway, she followed him, still wielding her makeshift weapon, delivering blow after blow. With another cry of pain, he turned toward the stairs, but she was ready for that. She drew back and landed a direct hit on his kidney. A strangled cry of pain let her know she'd delivered a punishing stroke.

His back arched, and his foot slipped from the top step. Panting for breath, she stood at the top of the stairwell and watched as he tumbled down the stairs. He landed at the bottom with a loud thud and lay there for a split second before he pushed to his feet. Slowly, he turned his head, gazed at her on the landing and shook his fist.

"This ain't over!"

She glared back at him and raised the broom again. With a muttered expletive, he hobbled to the door and rushed out into the night. Unsure what to do, she stood still, afraid to move. What if he came back? She might not be able to fight him off the next time. Her mind raced with thoughts of what she could do to protect herself and the babies. She knew she needed to call the police, but her frantic, chaotic thoughts kept her frozen in place. She was only able to move when she heard the cries of Emma and Ethan coming from their bedroom.

Turning, she ran to her bedroom, grabbed her cell phone and rushed back to the twins. By this time, they were both howling at the top of their lungs. She flipped the lock on the nursery's door and rushed to give each of the babies a swift kiss before she dialed in a call to nine-one-one.

The operator answered right away. "Nine-one-one. What is your emergency?"

"This is Holly Lee," she gasped. "I'm at Tumbling Creek Ranch on Ridge Road. A man just broke into my house."

"Is the man still there?"

"No. I was able to fight him off, and he ran out the front door."

"Where are you now?" the operator asked.

"I'm locked in one of the bedrooms upstairs with my niece and nephew."

"Help is on the way," she said. "Keep the door locked and stay there until you hear the officers arrive. I'll remain on the phone with you until they get there."

Holly reached out and gave each child a hug with her free arm as she continued to clutch the phone with her other hand to her ear. "How long is it going to be?"

"Don't worry," the operator said. "They're only a few minutes out. Is your front door unlocked?"

"I—I think so. That's the way the man left."

"Then just hang on and talk to me until the officers get there."

The soothing tone of the operator's voice calmed her as she tried to quiet the babies. "It's okay," she crooned as she planted a kiss on the head of each one. "Aunt Holly isn't going to let anything happen to you."

Emma's cries turned into a soft sob as she looked

up at her. Tears filled her big blue eyes, and she stuck her thumb in her mouth. Ethan held up his arms in invitation to be picked up. Holly wanted to grab them both up and hug them to her chest, but she still had the phone to her ear. Try as she might, she hadn't yet mastered the technique of picking both babies up at one time. How had her sister managed?

The thought of her sister brought tears to her eyes, and she looked down at the twins, who'd become so important to her in the last few weeks since her sister's and brother-in-law's deaths. Their children were the only family Holly had left. What if that man had hurt them tonight? The thought made her stomach roil.

"Ma'am, are you still there?" The operator's voice jerked her from her thoughts.

"Yes, I'm still here." She hesitated for a moment and breathed a sigh of relief. "I hear the police sirens now. I think they're almost here."

"They are. They should be inside your house in the next few minutes."

The sound of a car screeching to a halt in front of the house split the air, and then she heard the front door slam open, followed by footsteps pounding up the stairs. "Holly! Where are you?"

When she heard the familiar voice, her grip on the phone loosened, and she barely caught it before it slipped from her hand. The locked door rattled as the person on the other side tried to get in. "Holly! Are you in there? Open up."

Her arm dropped away from the protective hug around Ethan, and he erupted in cries. "Shh." She smiled as she shushed the babies and pulled the phone closer. "Someone's here now, and I'm going to hang up. Thank you for staying on the line with me."

"I'm glad I was able to help. Now, go let the police in."

Holly ended the call and took a deep breath before she walked to the door. When she reached to unlock it, she hesitated and bit down on her lip. She should have known he'd come, but she'd been so rattled that she hadn't expected him. She took a deep breath and opened the door to face the man she hadn't seen in ten years.

Cole raised his hand to pound again but stopped as he heard the lock click. Then the door eased open and Holly stood there. All he could do was stare at her. Of course, he'd seen her from a distance at her sister and brother-in-law's memorial service, and he'd seen her picture splashed across newspapers' front pages, television screens and social-media sites many times over the last several years. But this was the first time he'd had a chance to see her up close since she'd left for Nashville ten years ago to pursue her dream of becoming a country-music star. She hadn't changed that much. Her hair was a shade lighter, not quite the honey-blond color he remembered from their first day of school when they were children. There were also stress lines around her blue eyes, but that was to be expected.

With the release of her latest album, *Traces*, that had already gone platinum, he couldn't imagine the pressure of promotions and public appearances so soon after her sister's and brother-in-law's deaths. He'd seen her on a late-night talk show last week and had wondered how she was doing as he studied her body language.

Now, as they stared at each other, he had to remind himself that he was there in response to a nine-one-one call, not a personal one. After all, she'd never tried to contact him in all these years and apparently hadn't looked back when she left him for her big chance in Nashville. It had taken him years to move on, and he believed he had put all of his feelings for Holly behind him. He had to be careful and not let old resentments flare up or hurtful memories surface. He'd worked too hard to forget her for that to happen.

"Cole," she whispered. "Thank you for coming."

He took a step forward. "Holly, are you and the kids all right?"

She gave the crying babies another hug and nodded. "We're fine. Just had quite a scare. How did you get here so fast?"

"I woke up when the report came over my scanner, and I knew I was probably closer than any of our patrol cars. So I jumped out of bed and rushed over here. Which way did the intruder go?"

"He went out the front door, but I didn't hear a car." A sudden thought struck her, and her eyes grew wide. "Do you think he could still be outside?"

A grimace pulled at Cole's mouth as he pulled his cell phone from his pocket and tapped a number in. When Dispatch answered, he responded with orders. "Detective Jackson here. I'm at Tumbling Creek Ranch with the victim, but the intruder has left. I need the search team to sweep the area and make sure he's not hiding somewhere." He listened for a moment before he spoke again. "Ten-four. Let me know when they're on the way."

When he disconnected the call, he looked back at Holly and noticed the way her lips trembled.

"Do you think he might still be around?" she asked.

"I don't know. I just want to be sure. There's a patrol car on the way here now, but the search team should be along shortly. If he's here, they'll find him."

A sigh of relief escaped from her mouth, and a wobbly smile pulled at her lips. "Thank you, Cole."

He started to reply, but Ethan's cry distracted him. He stepped around her and walked over to the bed. "Hey, buddy, what's the matter?" Ethan held out his arms, and Cole scooped him up and held him close. "How you doing, little man? You've grown since I last saw you."

Holly watched as Cole jiggled the baby, calming his cries, and then she walked over and picked up Emma. They stood beside the cribs, each comforting one of the twins, and his eyes locked on her. "Now tell me what happened."

She took a deep breath and began to describe what had taken place in the bedroom. He listened as she talked, and he nodded from time to time. When he got to the part about how she'd used a broom as a weapon, he tried to smother his grin. He could just imagine the intruder's surprise when she'd gone on the offensive.

Just as she finished, he heard people calling out from downstairs. "Miss Lee? Where are you?"

"Up here," Cole called out.

The words were barely out of his mouth before two

uniformed officers, Zach Thomas and April Cantrell, appeared at the bedroom door. They stopped momentarily and stared at him holding one of the babies before they glanced at each other with confusion on their faces. Zach cleared his throat and nodded at him. "Detective Jackson, I didn't expect you to already be here."

"I live nearby," Cole replied and glanced back at Holly. "I've called for a search team, and I was just getting information about the break-in from Miss Lee. Why don't we go sit down, so we can get the official report?"

Holly cast an uncertain glance at the twins as if she didn't know what to do with them. With a smile, April stepped forward. "Why don't you let me take care of these precious babies while you talk to Detective Jackson and Officer Thomas?"

Holly hesitated for a moment. "Are you sure?"

April nodded. "I have two children of my own. I think I'm up to the job."

Reluctantly, Holly surrendered Emma to her, and Cole set Ethan back in his bed. "Let's talk downstairs," Cole said as he turned back to Holly.

She nodded and turned to lead the way from the room. As she stepped away, soft whimpers came from the direction of the crib, and she turned to see Ethan standing up and holding on to the railing around the bed. His mouth was pulled into a frown, and his eyes were filled with tears.

She started to go to him, but April shook her head. "I've got this. Go on and get the report filled out."

Holly bit down on her lip as if reluctant to leave the children, but after a moment, she turned and led the way downstairs to the den. When they were seated, Cole pulled a small notepad and pen from his pocket, then looked at Holly. "I know you've already told me once what happened, but I need you to tell me again, so I can make sure I have all the information. Concentrate and try to remember every detail."

Holly nodded and began to speak. Cole wrote as she described herself waking and not hearing the music over the baby monitor—and then everything that followed after to the point where she locked herself in the bedroom with the twins and called nine-one-one.

When she'd finished, Cole glanced back over the notes he'd taken while she'd been talking. Then he looked around the room. There didn't appear to be any evidence of a robbery. In fact, everything looked neat and in place. At first glance, it appeared that Holly had interrupted a kidnapping of her niece and nephew. A high ransom wouldn't be a problem for a wealthy music star. The fact that the intruder had turned the monitor off convinced Cole even more that this had been intended as a kidnapping, but there was no need to worry Holly at this point.

He flipped the notepad closed and took a deep breath. "So how long are you here for, Holly?"

Her shoulders tensed, and she clasped her hands in her lap. "Just a few days. I came home to clear the house out and put the ranch up for sale."

His eyes grew wide. "You're selling your father's ranch?"

She nodded. "Yes. With my schedule, I can't take care of it. I'd rather it belong to someone who will."

He didn't reply but looked to Officer Thomas, who

had a quizzical look on his face. "Zach, I guess you realize who Holly is."

Zach nodded. "Who doesn't know who Holly Lee is? Local girl who made it big in the country-music industry and one of the top-selling artists of the day. It's a pleasure to meet you, Miss Lee."

She smiled. "Thank you, Zach. I appreciate your help tonight."

"I was really sorry to hear about your sister's and brother-in-law's deaths. Was this their house?"

Holly nodded. "Yes. My sister and I grew up here. After my father died, Ruth and her husband, Michael, took over the property." She glanced back at the staircase. "The twins upstairs are their children."

He started to say something else, but Cole interrupted him. "I think we have all the information we need. I heard the search team drive up. Why don't you go help them?"

Zach nodded and pushed to his feet. "Will do. If that guy's still around, Miss Lee, we'll find him."

Holly smiled her thanks as Zach walked from the room and then turned back to face Cole, who sat in a chair facing her. For a moment, she didn't say anything. Then she cleared her throat. "How have you been?"

He gave a slight nod. "Fine. And you?"

She blinked back the tears that filled her eyes. "I just try to get through each day." She sat silent for a moment. "It still seems so unreal. I'll never forget the day I received that phone call from the Louisiana authorities telling me that Ruth and Michael's plane had crashed into Lake Pontchartrain."

Cole nodded. "I know. Michael had been so excited about taking Ruth on that weekend trip to New Orleans. I couldn't believe it ended so tragically. What's the latest with the investigation?"

She sighed and rubbed her hands over her eyes. "Nothing. They found the plane, but Ruth's and Michael's bodies weren't inside. No one has been able to find any trace of them. I had thought…maybe once we found them and had a funeral, I could get some closure. But now—" Her last words ended on a sob, and he reached out and grasped her hand.

"Don't think about that, Holly. Just be thankful the twins weren't with them."

She brushed the tears from her cheeks and straightened her shoulders. "You're right. I thank God every day that the twins were with me in Nashville for that weekend. If they'd been on that plane, they would have died, too. But I'm also thankful that Ruth and Michael had me in their will to be guardian if anything happened to both of them." Her eyes teared up again. "But who would have thought they'd die together?"

A sharp pang pierced his heart at the thought of Michael Whitson, his best friend ever since he could remember, and Michael's pretty wife, Ruth. He'd often wondered what they'd experienced when they knew their plane was going down. He swallowed and cleared his throat.

"When they recovered the plane, could they tell the cause of the crash?"

Holly shook her head. "No. The plane didn't have a black box to record anything, and they couldn't detect anything wrong with it. They haven't released the official findings, but I've been told they're leaning toward pilot error."

"What?" Cole exclaimed. "Michael was the most thorough pilot I've ever known."

"I know. It just seems so unreal. In the meantime, I'm trying to take care of the twins and prepare for my tour that's coming up this fall."

"Getting this place ready to sell must be another load of responsibility on top of that. Why bother with it now?"

"Maintaining the ranch when I don't live here would be a bigger responsibility. Something has to go, so it's going to be the ranch. I live three hundred miles away, and I'm too busy to keep things running here."

A flash of anger flared in him, and he pushed to his feet. "Yeah, I know. When you left Jackson Springs, you left for good. Now, with Ruth and Michael gone, there's nothing here for you anymore."

She rose and faced him. "I cut my ties with this place ten years ago."

The look on her face defused his anger, and he let out a long breath. "Yeah, you did. I guess I know that more than anybody, Holly. I'm sorry if I let old memories intrude on an official police call. I promise I won't do that again." He slipped the notepad back in his pocket. "Our department will do whatever it takes to keep you safe while you're here." He stopped and frowned. "It just dawned on me. You're here alone. Where is your security team? And your personal assistant?"

"I needed to get away from the press and just spend a few days by myself going through everything and deciding what needs to be kept for Emma and Ethan. I thought I could slip into town and fly under the radar without my security team. Mrs. Green, Ruth's housekeeper, has been helping me out with the children. My assistant is in Knoxville visiting with her family."

"We'll try to keep your presence under wraps, but it's clear now that someone knows you're here. Also, our report will be public record, so I imagine paparazzi will show up here tomorrow. Better get your security people on the job as soon as possible."

She nodded. "Thanks, Cole. I'll do that."

He wanted to say something else to her, but he couldn't find the words. Finally, he turned and headed for the door. Before he walked out, he turned to her. "Lock up well before you go to bed, and keep your cell phone handy in case your visitor comes back. I'll have patrol drive by here throughout the night to keep an eye out. You can call nine-one-one if you need anything."

He started to head to the door, but she called out to him. "Cole, it was good to see you again."

He wanted to turn back to her and tell her the same, but he couldn't. The words she'd spoken ten years ago were burned in his mind. She'd broken his heart and walked away as if he meant nothing to her.

Now all he could do was nod. Then he opened the door and walked out into the night. He stood on the porch after he'd closed the door on her—just as she had done when she tossed aside the love they shared and walked away from him.

He didn't think he could ever forgive her for that.

TWO

An hour later, the last police car had left, and Holly locked the door. She used to feel safe in this house, but that was when she was a child and her parents were still alive. Now, with Ruth gone, too, the house was a sad reminder of what had once been a happy home. She doubted if she would ever experience the feeling again that she'd had growing up here.

The house she'd bought in Nashville had proved to be just that—a house, not a home—since she was seldom there. She had a maid, a cook and a gardener who took care of everything, and sometimes it seemed more like a hotel than a place where she belonged. Then there was her security team who hovered over her everywhere she went and a driver who was well trained in tactical driving that helped to avoid fans intent on following her.

At the thought of her security team, she grimaced. Bert Conley, the head of the team, had been upset that she'd insisted on going to Jackson Springs by herself. He'd wanted to send some men with her, but she'd refused. Now she wished she'd given in. At least she wouldn't have felt so alone.

Thoughts of Cole hit her, and she closed her eyes. She hadn't expected to see him tonight. Of course, Ruth had told her that he was now a detective with the sheriff's department, but she was surprised that he'd come instead of letting someone else take the report.

For a few minutes, she stood there thinking about the man she'd known ever since she could remember. Cole Jackson, whose ancestors had founded Jackson Springs in the early 1800s, had been a part of her life since he declared himself her boyfriend in first grade. Through the years, that bond had grown into love that came into full bloom during high school.

Everybody in town had expected them to get married as soon as they graduated, but she'd had other plans. The country-music band that she and Cole had started had whetted her appetite for something bigger than local one-night gigs, and she'd wanted them to go to Nashville and try to make it. Cole, however, had no interest in leaving Jackson Springs. He had told her he expected to spend all his life there. That was when she knew they had different goals for the future, and she'd left to make it on her own.

And make it she had. Now she was at the top of the charts and booked on another tour. All she had to do was keep convincing herself that she'd gotten what she wanted. She'd thought she had, until Ruth's death made her realize how important family was. She missed her sister and the telephone calls that lasted for hours sometimes. Ruth had always been her compass to guide her, and now she was left to provide that for Ruth's children. The thought that she wasn't up to the task troubled her. She practically lived on a tour bus—what kind of life was that for two small children? Leaving them behind didn't seem like an option, either. She didn't want to see them just in snatches between tours. And what about other issues? She had become somewhat accustomed to the constant presence of someone, whether a paparazzo or a fan, bent on taking her picture. She didn't want Emma and Ethan exposed to that. It was overwhelming, even when the people on the other end of it were well-intentioned. And when they weren't…

Tonight had just reinforced those concerns. The thought of the baby carrier the man wore sent chills down her spine. There could only be one reason for that—he had come to kidnap the twins. She could tell from the way Cole had avoided her gaze when she told him about the intruder having one that he thought so, too. This was no ordinary robbery. It had to have been an attempted kidnapping. Nothing appeared to have been touched in the house, and the intruder's attention seemed to have been focused on the twins.

A shiver ran up her spine, and she wrapped her arms around her waist. She needed to check all the doors once more before going back to bed, but she wasn't going to turn the lights off. She hurried to take care of that before heading back upstairs.

Five minutes later, she tiptoed back into the nursery. Emma's quiet snuffle drifted across the room, and she smiled. She was grateful April had been one of the responding officers tonight. She'd been able to calm both children and get them asleep by the time she had to leave. Now they both slept soundly.

She, however, wasn't willing to go back to her

room and leave them. She turned the lock on the door, grabbed a quilt from the closet and settled herself in the rocking chair. As she pulled the cover up over herself, the memory of trying to ward off their attacker returned, and she blinked back tears. She had no idea where the strength came from to do that. It had taken over her body and filled her with a fierce resolve to protect her family. She could only hope that it would be enough to keep them safe—at least for tonight. Settling down in the chair, she closed her eyes and tried to go to sleep.

Hours later, she still sat there wide-eyed and unable to relax. All through the night, she'd watched the glow from the "Hickory Dickory Dock" clock on the wall, as the hands shaped like mice displayed the time. Now it was 6:00 a.m. and still too early for Mandy to be up, but she needed to speak with her.

Easing quietly from her chair, she unlocked the door and walked back to her bedroom. Once inside, she pulled her cell phone from her robe pocket and dialed the number of her assistant. It rang several times before Mandy answered.

"Hello." The gravelly tone of Mandy's sleep-filled voice came over the phone.

"Mandy, this is Holly. I've had a problem here in Jackson Springs. I know you're visiting your parents and that today's your mother's birthday, but I wondered if you could come today when the party is over. I really need your help."

She could hear the squeak of bedsprings as Mandy sat up. "What's wrong, Holly?"

The fear she'd felt during the night returned as she related what had transpired. When she'd finished, she spoke again. "I shouldn't have come here alone. I need you to help me with the twins, and I need the security team in place."

"I'll get in touch with Bert right away, and I'll be there tonight." Mandy spoke with the efficiency she'd displayed ever since Holly had hired her three years ago. "Do you want me to call Aiden, too? He's in Chicago today finishing up the details of your concert there."

Holly bit down on her lip at the mention of her manager, Aiden Hudson, and thought for a moment before she responded. "You can call him to update him on the situation, but tell him to get everything worked out in Chicago. If you can get here and Bert can get security in place, we should be okay."

"Okay, I'm on it." Mandy paused for a moment, then spoke. "Are you sure you're all right? I can skip my mother's birthday party if you'd like."

"No, don't do that. Enjoy being with your family. Just get here afterward, and please apologize to your folks for me. I'm sorry to pull you away from your visit. I promise I'll make it up to you with more time off."

Mandy gave a soft chuckle. "No need for apologies, Holly. You are way too good to me, anyway, and they know that. Don't worry. I'll leave after the dinner party tonight."

Smiling, Holly disconnected the call, checked on the twins to make sure they were still sleeping and headed downstairs. Ten minutes later, she poured her first cup of coffee and carried it into the den. She was just about to take a sip when she heard a vehicle stop in front of the house. She eased over to the window and pulled the curtain back to peer outside. An unmarked police car sat in the driveway. As she watched, Cole climbed out and walked up the front steps.

She waited for him to knock, but when he didn't, she walked to the door and opened it. He stood bent over on the porch, his attention directed to the lock on the door. He gasped in surprise at the sight of her, his body jerking. He staggered backward. Holly tried not to smile, but the look of shock on his face reminded her of how he'd looked when they were children and she'd mistaken a copperhead for a milk snake and picked it up.

At the sound of her laughter, he clenched his jaw and straightened to his full height. "What's so funny?" he growled.

"You are," she said. "The expression on your face reminded me of the time I picked up that copperhead."

A small grin tugged at the corner of his mouth, and his shoulders relaxed. "Yeah. I remember that day. I thought you were going to be bitten before I could get to you."

A warm rush filled her as she remembered how he'd raced to rescue her. "You always looked out for me, Cole."

He pursed his lips but didn't say anything. Finally, she cleared her throat and spoke again. "What are you doing skulking around on my front porch so early in the morning?"

He took a deep breath as if to clear his thoughts and gave a slight nod toward the door. "I wanted to check out the door again and see if I overlooked anything last night to determine how your visitor got in. I thought I'd do it before you got up so that I wouldn't disturb you."

"And did you find anything?"

He shook his head. "No. The lock doesn't look like it's been jimmied, and all the other doors were locked. You said your intruder pulled this door open when he ran out. Are you sure you locked it before you went to bed last night?"

"Yes. I remember testing it twice to make sure it was secure."

Cole rubbed the back of his neck and frowned. "None of the windows had been opened or broken. He had to come in this way. Maybe he had a key."

Her eyes grew wide. "How would that be possible?"

Cole shrugged. "I don't know. Maybe he's a former employee who worked on the ranch for Michael or for your dad. He might have found a key to the house and kept it. Or he could have picked the lock. A good burglar can do that easily."

"We both know he wasn't here to rob me, Cole. He wanted the twins."

His forehead wrinkled as he studied the lock and then nodded. "Yeah. I think you're right."

Although it was early summer, there was still a nip in the air in the mornings. Holly shivered and wrapped her arms around her waist. "While you're trying to make sense of this, would you like a cup of coffee?"

Cole's mouth opened as if he was about to speak. Then he exhaled and shook his head. "No, thanks. I don't want to bother you."

At his clear reluctance to come inside, a sharp pain pierced her heart and she winced. What had happened to them? They'd been best friends since childhood, and now they were barely able to tolerate being in the same vicinity. Things might have ended badly for them in the romance department, but it was time they salvaged their friendship.

"It's no trouble, Cole," she said. "We ought to be able to share a cup of coffee for old times' sake."

An undecided look flashed in his eyes, and she was sure he was going to tell her no. Instead, he nodded. "You're right. I'd love a cup of coffee."

She grinned and stepped back for him to enter the house. "Good. Come on back to the kitchen."

He followed her through the house without speaking and stopped just inside the kitchen door. She motioned for him to have a seat at the table. She refilled her cup and poured one for him before she turned back and set them on the table.

"Black. No sugar or cream," she said with a smile.

He picked up the spoon she'd placed on the saucer and began to stir the hot coffee. He smiled as he glanced up at her. "You remembered how I take my coffee."

"And why wouldn't I?" she said with a laugh. "We've probably consumed gallons of coffee together through the years."

He chuckled and nodded. "Yeah. I guess we have." They sat in silence for a few minutes as they sipped from their cups. Then he set his mug down and lifted his head to stare at her. "How have you been, Holly? Other than losing your sister and Michael, I mean."

She shrugged. "Okay, I guess. I miss Ruth. No

matter where I was or what I was doing, we talked every day on the phone. Sometimes, I pick up my cell phone to call her before I remember that she isn't going to answer."

"I know how you feel." His gaze drifted around the kitchen. "I really miss coming here. I would stop by on my way to work several times a week, and Michael and I would have a cup of coffee together. Ruth used to join us, but after they adopted the twins she was busy all the time."

Holly smiled at the memory of how excited Ruth had been the day she called to tell her that the adoption had finally gone through and they were picking up Emma and Ethan that afternoon. "She went through so much with all the in vitro treatments she had, trying to get pregnant. But she said all her disappointments disappeared the first time she saw the twins."

Cole picked up his cup and stared at her over the top. "And now you have them. How have you been dealing with it?"

Holly shrugged. "Okay, I guess, but I have a lot of help. At first, I thought I couldn't do it. My lifestyle doesn't lend itself to raising children. I thought about terminating my rights and letting someone else adopt them, but then I knew I couldn't. They are Ruth's children, and they're all the family I have left. And after what happened last night… It makes me wonder why on earth I thought I could come here alone and take care of them."

Cole set his coffee back down. "You did a great job protecting them last night. But it would probably help if you had someone here with you."

She nodded. "That's why I called my assistant to cut her stay at her parents' home short and come help me. I hated to do that, but I'll make it up to her."

"What about security? I know you have a team. I think they should be here, too."

"They will be soon."

Cole took one last drink from his cup, set it down and pushed to his feet. "Good. I'm glad you're going to be protected. I'll have the officers continue to patrol by here, and if you'll give me your cell phone number, I'll have my partner get in touch with you if we turn up anything about your intruder."

Holly realized he had just let her know he wouldn't be getting in touch himself or seeing her again before she left. Trying to keep her voice steady, she recited her number and watched as he programmed it into his phone. Then, without speaking again, he rose to leave.

Unable to let him leave like that, she followed him to the front door. Just as he reached for the doorknob, she called out to him. "Cole, wait."

He stopped and faced her. "What is it?"

She licked her lips and clasped her hands in front of her. "Ever since you arrived last night, you've acted like I'm just another victim of a crime you're investigating. Cole, we've known each other since we were children, and for years I was closer to you than I was to anybody else. I don't want us to be reserved with each other. I would like for us to be friends again."

He stared at her with a skeptical look on his face. "Friends? How can we do that? You broke my heart, Holly. I don't have any desire to be friends with you again."

She blinked back tears. "I know I did, but that was ten years ago. Surely you've moved on by now. Ruth told me once that you were serious about a woman from Gatlinburg."

He shook his head. "It didn't work out. There's nobody in my life right now. You, on the other hand, are featured on magazine covers all the time on the arm of a handsome singer or movie star at red-carpet events."

"That's all arranged by my publicity team," she responded. "Most of the men I go out with are less interested in getting to know me and more concerned that I'm going to get more attention from the paparazzi than they are."

Although she'd hoped to lighten the atmosphere with that final comment, he didn't smile. "Sounds like you have a really tough life. But it's just what you always wanted. You left Jackson Springs to find it, and now you've come back to rid yourself of the last hold that this place has on you. I hope you're able to find a buyer right away."

The flat tone of his voice stung her. "The Realtor doesn't think she'll have trouble selling the ranch. Its location is a real asset. It's in a valley surrounded by the Smokies, which makes it a prime example of a vacation home. So once I get everything cleaned out, the twins and I will be on our way back to Nashville."

He nodded. "Have a safe trip."

With that, he turned and strode toward the front door. When she heard it close, a sad feeling engulfed her. She hadn't expected seeing Cole again would be so hard. She was being truthful when she'd said he was the best friend she'd ever had, and lately she'd come to miss that.

With a sigh, she picked up the coffee cups and carried them to the sink. Cole had no interest in being her friend, and she would just have to accept that. After all, she had no one to blame but herself.

At least she knew he would do his best to keep her and the babies safe—for the twins' sake and in honor of Ruth and Michael's memory, if nothing else. That was what mattered the most. Cole might not trust her anymore, but the twins were counting on her, dependent on her in every way.

She wouldn't—couldn't—let them down.

Cole didn't look back as he drove away from Tumbling Creek Ranch. Once, it had been a second home to him, but now he felt like a stranger there. He'd held on to his attachment to it while Ruth and Michael were alive, but now it was Holly's, and she was going to sell it.

That shouldn't have surprised him, but somehow it did. How could she get rid of the land that her father had loved so much? But then, she had severed all connections with everything in this place, except for her sister, when she left years ago.

He clenched his jaw as he thought back to that time and how he'd felt when she'd broken off their engagement and moved to Nashville. To her credit, she'd begged him to go with her, to stay in the band that they'd started together. But in his heart, he knew he didn't have the talent that she had, and he also didn't have the dream of making it in the music industry. He supposed, in the end, their relationship had turned out the only way it could. She'd left, and he'd stayed.

Now she said she wanted to be friends, but that was never going to happen. He could just hope that the ranch would sell right away and she'd be gone. Back to Nashville and out of his life for good.

Shaking the troubling thoughts from his head, he directed his attention back to the road. With summer just having begun, tourists had flooded into Jackson Springs to spend some time in the Smokies. The sight of so many cars on the road made him smile as he drove into town. Ten minutes later, he walked down the hall of the sheriff's department and entered his office.

His partner, Dan Welch, had the day off, and Cole settled behind his desk to do some paperwork he'd been putting off. He tried to push his conversation with Holly from his mind and forced himself to concentrate on the papers in front of him. He had no idea how long he'd worked and was shocked to look up a while later and see that it was almost lunchtime. He stood up and stretched his back, which had grown stiff while he was hunched over his desk, and was about to leave his office when the phone rang. The light on the base showing the various lines coming into the office indicated a call on line one from the receptionist. He picked up the receiver and answered. "Hey, Brenda. What's up?"

"You have a call on line one from a young woman, Cole. I'll connect you," she answered.

Almost immediately, he heard the click that told him he'd been connected to the caller. "Detective Jackson speaking." For a moment, he didn't think anyone was there, and then he heard a throat clearing.

He waited for someone to say something, but there was silence on the line. "Can I help you?"

"Yes," a voice replied but didn't say anything else.

He frowned as he tried to determine if he'd ever heard the voice before and decided he hadn't. It was definitely a woman's voice. And she sounded afraid.

"What do you need?"

The caller took a deep breath. "I think they're trying to kill me, because I know too much."

Her voice trembled, and Cole sat up straight in his chair. "Who's trying to kill you, and what do you know about?"

"I don't know all their names, but…" She paused, and when she spoke again, her voice was laced with panic. "He's…he's found me."

"Where are you?" Cole asked. "I'll come for you."

"No! I have to go!"

With those words, the call disconnected. "Ma'am, where are you?" he yelled into the phone, but there was no answer.

He punched the button that connected him to Brenda's phone, and she answered right away. "Cole, do you need something?"

"Have our tech guys see if they can find out where that last phone call came from, and tell them it's urgent. Let me know as soon as they have something."

"I'll get right on it," she said before ending the call.

For the next fifteen minutes, Cole paced the floor in his office as conflicting thoughts ran through his head. What if the girl on the phone had been lying? Some people enjoyed giving a false police report, and she could be one of them. On the other hand, though, she had sounded really frightened.

When the phone rang again, he grabbed the receiver. "Brenda? Any word on the call?"

"Yes. The call came from a cell phone and pinged off the tower near the old water plant. They placed her somewhere in the vicinity of that mall on Sturgis Road."

"I'm on it," Cole said before he slammed the phone down and headed out the door.

He knew he was probably on a wild-goose chase. How could he possibly identify a girl when he'd only heard her voice? Something in the way she spoke, though, told him that she was serious about being in danger. He'd heard fear in people's voices before, and hers definitely told him she was afraid.

Whether or not he'd be able to find her, he had to try.

THREE

Getting the twins ready for the day was a full-time job, and Holly wondered again how her sister had done it. Holly usually had someone to help her, but the nanny she'd hired had recently quit, and Mandy hadn't been able to find another one yet. Maybe while Mandy was here she could work on that.

Thankfully, two members of her security team had arrived. With one at the front of the house and one behind it, she felt safer. But there was another problem. She needed to go to the grocery store.

She stepped out onto the front porch and was met by Todd Bingham, who'd been on her security team for about two years. "Miss Lee, is there something I can do for you?"

"Yes, Todd. I hate to ask you, but could you and Ray take me to the grocery store? I need to do some shopping."

Todd frowned. "I'm not sure you need to go out in public after what happened last night."

"It'll be okay. Evidently, the break-in hasn't been discovered by the media yet. If it had been, we'd have reporters all over the place. So let's go before they find out. I may not have another chance."

He looked like he wasn't convinced, but he raised his walkie-talkie to his mouth. "Ray, we're going to town. Bring the car around."

"Thanks, Todd," Holly said. "Come inside and get one of the twins, and I'll bring the other one. We need to put their stroller in the car, too."

"Yes, ma'am," he replied as he followed her into the house.

Ten minutes later, Ray pulled the car to a stop in front of the supermarket inside the Sturgis Road Mall. Holly pulled the baseball cap she wore lower on her head and slipped on her sunglasses before she stepped from the SUV. With Todd's help, they settled Emma and Ethan in the double stroller.

Todd turned to Ray. "Park the car and then wait out front. If you see anything suspicious, call me."

Ray nodded. "Yes, sir."

As they walked toward the automatic doors at the store's entrance, Holly hoped if anyone was looking she, Todd and the children would look like a normal family coming to do some shopping. Once inside, Todd grabbed a shopping cart and they headed toward the first aisle.

No one seemed to pay them any attention. She just wished Todd would relax more. His gaze darted here and there, and every time they approached someone, he would place his body between her and the other person.

"Todd," she whispered. "Relax."

"I'll relax when we're back at the ranch, ma'am."

She laughed at the flat tone of his voice and stopped

in front of the cereal that the children liked. She was about to pick up a box when something caught her eye at the other end of the aisle, and she turned her head to see a young woman staring at them.

At first, Holly thought she might be a reporter, but the more she studied her the more she thought that couldn't be. Her brown hair hung down to her shoulders, and it looked as if it hadn't been brushed all day. Even from far away, Holly could see the red streaks around her eyes. They seemed to stand out, especially since her face was so pale. She gave the appearance of someone who hadn't slept in days.

The young woman's gaze flickered from her to the babies and then back to Holly. There was something in her eyes that sent cold chills down Holly's spine. Who was she, and why was she staring at the twins so intently?

Suddenly the woman whirled and disappeared down the next aisle. Holly stood there a moment, wondering what that was all about. Todd, who'd been looking the other way, evidently hadn't seen her, and Holly didn't say anything. The girl probably recognized Holly and was just shocked to see a country-music star buying groceries.

Shaking off her discomfort, she tossed the cereal in the cart and pushed the stroller toward the end of the aisle. Todd followed with the cart. When she rounded the end, she looked about in hopes of catching another glimpse of the strange woman, but she was nowhere to be seen. Maybe Holly was overreacting thanks to nerves that were still fragile from her experience the night before. With a shake of her head, she pushed the stroller toward the produce section and came to a stop in front of a display of bananas. Emma and Ethan spied their favorite fruit stacked up and began to point.

Holly laughed and chucked each one under the chin. "Don't worry. I'm going to get you some."

She was just about to pick up one of the bunches when she heard a cry at the end of the aisle at the back of the produce section. She froze in place and turned a startled gaze in that direction. A man lay on the floor, and a crowd had begun to gather around him.

"Call an ambulance. Does anyone know CPR?" someone called out.

Todd glanced at Holly. "I know CPR. I need to go help him."

Holly nodded. "Go on. See what you can do."

Todd rushed over to the prostrate figure and dropped down on his knees beside the unconscious man. He leaned over and examined him for a moment before he looked up. "He's breathing on his own," he announced, loud enough for Holly to hear him. "I'll just watch him until the paramedics get here."

Holly took a step closer to the drama that was playing out on the floor of the supermarket and stared at the man who lay there. The observing crowd was growing, and it looked like every customer in the store had congregated in the area. With the thought that Todd could handle the situation, she turned back to the twins.

Later, she would remember that she had only looked away for not more than a few seconds. But that was all the time someone had needed. The space where the stroller had sat was now empty, and the twins were nowhere in sight.

She looked around in panic before the first scream ripped from her throat. "My children! Someone's taken my children!"

Todd came barreling through the crowd toward her, but she was already running to the front of the store. "Did you see someone leave with two children in a stroller?" she yelled at the checkout girl.

Her eyes grew wide, and she nodded. "A man just pushed a stroller out the front door."

Holly ran outside and plowed into a man who was standing still and staring at something behind her. She looked over her shoulder and gasped to see Ray lying on the sidewalk. Blood ran from his head. Part of her wanted to run and check on him—but the children needed her more. She turned to look in the opposite direction, and that was when she saw a man running down the street, pushing the stroller.

"Stop that man!" she screamed and took off in pursuit, but the man only increased his speed.

Holly realized that Todd was racing beside her as they tried to close the distance between them and the kidnapper. Suddenly, Todd's feet went out from under him, and he fell to the pavement. Holly didn't stop to check on him. She couldn't let the man take her children.

She closed the gap between them and screamed at the top of her lungs. "Stop! Give me my children!"

The man looked over his shoulder and glared at her with an evil look that she didn't think she would ever forget. And then, without warning, he gave the stroller a push. Holly screamed as the stroller holding Emma and Ethan rolled into the street and into the path of an oncoming car.

Cole scanned the crowd of people milling around in front of the Sturgis Road Mall. He didn't know what had possessed him to think he could find a woman that he didn't know in the middle of this crowded street. She could be any of the women he was passing. But anyone who sounded as scared as the voice on the phone had should show some physical evidence of fear, and he searched the faces of every woman he met to see if he could detect anything.

As he approached the mall's supermarket, he was close to giving up, but then he spotted a group of people just ahead on the sidewalk. When he got closer, he saw that a man lay there unconscious. Blood ran from his head.

He pushed into the group and flashed his badge. "Sheriff's department. What happened?"

A young man, who looked like he might be a college student, spoke up. "I saw it all. This guy was just standing here like he was waiting for someone. Then this other guy ran by and hit him on the head. He didn't even stop."

"Did you see where the attacker went?"

The boy shook his head. "No. I squatted down and tried to help this injured man. I did call nine-one-one, though."

"Good," Cole said. He was about to say something else when the door to the supermarket opened and a man ran out, pushing a double baby stroller.

From where he stood, he could see two blond

heads bobbing from inside the stroller as the man sped away. Cole frowned. The man's behavior seemed a little suspicious—but Cole hadn't seen anything to justify stopping him. He'd barely caught a glimpse of the children in the stroller, but they seemed unharmed. Maybe the guy was just in a hurry.

Cole was about to direct his attention back to the man on the ground when a shrill scream split the air. Startled, he looked up to see Holly burst out of the store and then run in the same direction as the fleeing man. Her agonized cry for the man to give her the children sliced through him, and he jumped to his feet and ran after her.

Cole kept his eyes on the stroller and willed his legs to move faster. To Holly's left a man that he guessed was one of her security team ran beside her. Cole saw the crack in the sidewalk but, evidently, Holly's bodyguard didn't. He caught his toe on the protruding concrete, and the next minute, he was down on the ground directly in Cole's path.

Cole took a flying leap over the man's prone figure and sped on right behind Holly. Then his stomach clenched as he saw the abductor give the stroller a hard shove toward the street. Holly let out a loud scream as the twins rolled directly into the path of an oncoming car.

He knew he had only seconds to react, and he responded without thinking, racing toward the stroller, which had come to a stop. Loud wails erupted from the children as they wiggled in their seats, but he didn't have time to comfort them as his hands fastened on the stroller's handle.

Out of the corner of his eye, he realized the car

was about to hit them, and he gave the stroller another hard shove. It rolled to the curb and came to a
stop just before Cole felt the impact. The breath left
his body as he was thrown up into the air and landed
with a crash on the hood of the car. The last thing
he remembered before losing consciousness was the
driver's frightened expression staring at him through
the windshield and the sound of Holly screaming his
name in the background.

When Cole opened his eyes, he lay still trying to
figure out what had happened to him. He frowned as
he recalled running after the twins and their kidnapper. And then he remembered the car and his attempt
to get the stroller out of the way. His heart dropped
to the pit of his stomach, and he swallowed. Had he
been successful, or had Emma and Ethan been hurt?

There was a rustling sound next to his bed as
someone came to stand beside him, and he turned
his head toward the person. He could hardly believe
it when Holly bent over him and placed her cool hand
on his forehead.

"You're awake." Her voice trembled as she stared
down at him.

"The twins?" he gasped as he tried to push up on
his elbows. "Are they all right?"

Her hands connected with his shoulders, and she
gently pushed him back down onto his back. "They're
fine, Cole, and alive because of what you did. How
can I ever thank you?"

His Adam's apple bobbed as he tried to calm the
way his heart raced at her touch. "There's no need
for thanks. I was just doing my job."

A skeptical look crossed her face, and she shook her head. "You did your job well, but I think it was more than that. You love those children. I saw it in your eyes last night when you were holding Ethan. And you put your life in danger to save them."

He stared up at her. "Where are they now?"

"On their way home with my security team. Mrs. Green, the housekeeper, called her daughter to come help with the twins, so they're taken care of. I wanted to stay here with you until I was sure that you were okay."

The mention of her security team brought to mind the fall that one of them had taken. "I saw your bodyguard fall. How is he?"

"Todd's okay, just a skinned knee. Ray didn't suffer any major injuries, either."

Cole frowned. "Who's Ray?"

"My other bodyguard. He was waiting outside the store for us and someone hit him on the head right before we ran from the store."

He recalled seeing the man lying on the sidewalk, and he nodded. "I got there right after he'd been knocked out. I was beside him when you ran out the door."

She smiled. "I'm so glad you followed." Her smile disappeared as her eyebrows drew down into a slight frown. "I don't understand, though. What were you doing there?"

He took a deep breath and told her about the strange phone call he'd gotten and how it had pinged off a tower nearby. "I don't know how I thought I'd find her, though. I have no idea what she looks like. She could be…" He stopped speaking when he noticed how her eyes had grown wide. "What's the matter?"

"There was a woman in the supermarket. She was standing at the end of an aisle staring at us. There was something about her that frightened me. Do you think she could be the woman who called you?"

He thought about it and then shook his head. "I don't know, but I can't find out anything lying in this bed. I need to check in with the station."

"The sheriff and two deputies were here earlier, but when the doctor told them you don't have any broken bones or head injuries, just some bruises that will heal with time, they left. The sheriff said for you to go home when you were discharged, and he'd talk to you about how much time you need to take off to recover."

"I don't need any time off. I need to get to work." He started to throw the covers back, but suddenly he realized while he'd been unconscious someone had changed him into a hospital gown. His gaze darted around the room. "Where are my clothes? I've got to get out of here."

She laid a restraining hand on his shoulder as he pushed up into a sitting position. "Cole, please lie back down. Your body has had quite a traumatic shock."

He took a deep breath and shook his head. "You don't understand, Holly. Last night, you fought off an intruder in the twins' bedroom. Today, they were abducted from a supermarket. I have to find out who that is. To top it off, I get a strange phone call from a frightened woman, and you see a stranger staring at Emma and Ethan. I've got to find out what's going on."

"Cole," she whispered, and he looked up to see that her face had gone pale. "You're scaring me. Why would anyone want to harm the twins?"

Regret that he'd frightened her washed over him, and he reached for her hand. "Holly, you are a very wealthy woman. A kidnapper would know that you'd pay any amount of money to get them back. We can't let this situation get to that point."

"B-but what can we do?" Tears began to roll down her cheeks, and her shoulders shook. "I can't lose them. They're all the family I have left."

His thumb stroked her knuckles as he spoke in a soothing tone. "I know, and I'm going to make sure they stay safe. Whatever's going on, I promise I will find out and protect them."

She wiped at her tears with her free hand and tried to smile. "Thank you, Cole. I know you will. I'm just thankful that you're here."

He bit down on his lip as he released her hand. "Now, how about you find a nurse, so that I can get my clothes, and we'll get out of here."

A nurse entered the room at that moment. He could tell by the amused look on her face that she had overheard him asking for his clothes. She smiled and wagged her finger at him. "Oh, no, you don't. The doctor wants to see you now that you're awake, and he'll decide if you can leave or not."

Cole's eyebrows arched, and he shook his head. "I'm fine. I've had worse mishaps in my line of work. I need to get out of here."

Holly propped her hands on her hips and rolled

her eyes as she glanced at the nurse. "He's always been a stubborn one. It may take some persuasion to keep him here."

The nurse laughed and stopped beside the bed. "I'm used to patients wanting out of here. But, Detective Jackson, we need to make sure you're okay before we release you. So settle down, and the doctor will be in to see you shortly. He'll let you know when you can be released."

Cole huffed and settled back on the bed as he mumbled something to himself. Holly couldn't help but grin. "Stubborn. That's what he is."

He glared up at her. "As if you're not."

The nurse rearranged the blanket over him and smiled. "Is there anything else I can get for you right now?"

Cole shook his head. "Just a get-out-of-jail-free card if you happen to have one."

She laughed and shook her head. "I'm afraid I don't have that, but I can bring you something to eat."

He shook his head. "I'm not hungry."

Holly bent down and stared in his face. "It's late afternoon now. Did you have lunch today?"

"No."

"Well then, you need to eat something." She turned to the nurse. "Can you get him a sandwich or maybe some soup?"

The nurse smiled. "I'll be glad to see what we have."

Cole raised himself up on his elbows and glared at Holly. "I told you I don't want…"

She smiled. "Oh, quit being a grouch. All we want to do is help you."

The nurse nodded. "That's right, Detective Jackson. Miss Lee hasn't left your side since you were brought in. You're fortunate to have someone who cares about you like that."

He looked up at Holly, and his heart thudded. "W-we're old friends," he finally said. "We've known each other since we were children."

"Well, it's good to have a friend like that." Then she turned and walked to the door. "I'll be back in a few minutes."

They watched her go, and then Holly looked back down at him. "Is there anything I can get for you? Another blanket or a drink of water?"

He shook his head. "No, thanks. I'm fine. I don't need any help," he grumbled.

She bit her lip and sat back down in the chair beside the bed. The silence between them grew heavy, and with each breath he took, he regretted the angry tone in his voice. He'd always been able to tell when she was sad. He could see it in the way her shoulders slumped now. And he had done that.

As he lay there watching her, she turned her head and stared out the window. Last night, she had asked him to be her friend again, and he had refused. The truth was that he wanted that friendship back more than anything he'd wanted in a long time. A bond had been forged between them years ago, and being away from each other for the past few years hadn't destroyed that. He doubted if anything ever would. The plans they'd had as teenagers hadn't come to pass, but they could still be there for each other. Just like she was for him right now.

"Holly," he whispered.

She wiped at her eyes before she turned back to face him. "What?"

"I'm really glad you're here."

Her chin trembled. "I'm glad I'm here, too. I'm so sorry you were hurt today because of me."

He frowned and shook his head. "It wasn't your fault. You had no idea someone was going to follow you to the store to try to kidnap the twins."

"I know, but I knew we'd had a break-in last night. And I knew better than to come to Jackson Springs without security in the first place. If I had planned better, none of this would have happened."

"You don't know that," he said.

"I do," she protested. "You know I've always been bound and determined to do everything my way. Well, I did, and it almost proved disastrous for Emma and Ethan."

He turned on his side so that his body was facing her and reached for her hand. "You can't blame yourself for this. I know you've been through some frightening experiences since you've been in town, but I'm going to do everything in my power to see that nothing happens to you or those children as long as you're here."

She smiled, and his stomach clenched at how beautiful she was. "Thank you, Cole. I appreciate that."

He cleared his throat and tightened his grip on her hand. "And, Holly, I'm sorry I refused your offer of friendship last night. I realize now that we'll always be friends and have each other's best interests at heart."

She stared at him for a moment before she spoke.

"Yes, Cole. We will." She let her gaze drift over his face, and then she smiled. "It's good to see you. I've missed you."

"I've missed you, too, Holly."

They didn't say anything else, and Cole knew there was no need for words. A lot had happened to both of them in the ten years since they'd parted, and they weren't those two young people who had once loved each other. But it felt so good to have his friend back, and he was never going to lose touch with her again.

FOUR

Holly was sitting at the desk in the den the next morning when she heard the familiar sound of Todd's footsteps in the hall. She stared at the doorway and waited for him to appear. When he did, he clasped his hands in front of him and directed his no-nonsense gaze toward her. For a moment, she had the fleeting thought that she'd rarely seen the man smile. On the few occasions that she had, the smile had always disappeared almost before it began.

"Todd?" she said. "Can I help you with something?"

He shook his head. "No, ma'am. Detective Jackson and two other men are here to see you. Do you want me to let them come in?"

She nodded. "Yes, of course."

Todd turned back to the hall as she rose from her chair. Cole stepped into the room, and she let her gaze rake over him. She'd expected him to have some bruises from being hit by the car yesterday, but nothing was visible. Before she could speak, two other men followed him into the den. One had salt-and-pepper hair and looked to be about fifty years old while the other looked like a college kid. He was dressed in black jeans and a black T-shirt with the word *Attitude*, the name of a rock band, plastered across the front. Several leather thongs with silver charms circled his neck, and leather bracelets covered both wrists.

"Good morning, Holly," Cole said. He turned to the men with him and pointed to the older one first. "This is Dan Welch, my partner, and this guy—" he paused as he pointed to the younger one "—is Jason Freeman. He's our sketch artist."

Holly smiled and motioned for them to come in. "I'm delighted to meet you. Please be seated, and I'll have Mrs. Green bring some coffee."

Cole shook his head. "No need for that. We just wanted to follow up on the incident yesterday."

Holly regarded him for a moment before she spoke. "When were you released from the hospital?"

He grinned. "This morning. Dan came and got me since my car was still parked at the Sturgis Road Mall. We brought Jason along because we thought as long as we're following up we ought to get a sketch of the young woman you saw in the store. Do you think you can describe her?"

She thought for a moment before she nodded. "I think I can." She glanced at Jason. "You can make a sketch from what a person describes?"

He beamed and nodded. "I'll do my best."

He opened a sketch pad that he was holding and pulled a pencil from his pocket. Holly studied him as he prepared to begin the drawing. He looked so much like hundreds of other kids who'd come to Nashville, hoping to hit it big in the music industry. In reality, only a few succeeded. She was thankful that she'd been one who had.

"Tell me, Jason," she said. "Are you a musician?"

His face flushed a bit. "Yes, ma'am. I play with a group of guys. Nothing like what your band, Ilex, does, but we stay busy with local gigs."

"Are you a roots-rock group?"

He tilted his head to one side and grinned. "How'd you guess?"

She looked back at his shirt. "Your Attitude shirt gave you away. Have you ever met Keith Jefferson?"

The pencil slipped from his fingers, and he stared up at her with a surprised look on his face. "The lead singer of the group? No way, but I wish I could."

She laughed. "Well, maybe you can come to Nashville sometime. Keith's my neighbor, and he's very friendly with his fans."

Jason's mouth gaped open, and he shook his head in awe. "Wow! I can't believe you know Keith Jefferson. My band members are gonna be blown away when I tell them."

"Well, we're here on police business, Jason," Cole interrupted in a sharp tone. "So, if you'd get on with it, I'd appreciate it."

"Yes, sir." Jason's face flushed as he sat up straighter in his chair. "Now, Miss Lee, let's see what you remember."

An hour later, Holly stared down at the sketch she held and shook her head in disbelief. "I can't believe you were able to do this. I didn't think I was describing her well, but you've captured her image perfectly. How did you do that?"

Jason glanced down at his drawing and shrugged.

"I don't know. I thought your descriptions were very easy to follow."

She handed the sketch to Cole. "This is the woman I saw in the supermarket. Do you recognize her?"

He shook his head and handed it to Dan, who studied it for a moment before returning it to Jason. "Can't say that I've ever seen her. We'll put her picture out to all our units and to other law enforcement in the area. Maybe one of them will spot her or recognize her as someone they know."

"Can't you put this in the newspaper and ask anyone to call if they see her?" Holly asked.

"We could," Cole said, "but as far as we know, she's done nothing illegal. We don't want to scare her off. For now, we'll just say she's wanted as a possible witness to a crime and use our resources to hunt for her quietly."

Holly glanced from Cole to Dan before she nodded. "Okay. Is there anything else I can do?"

Dan scooted to the edge of his seat and stared at her. "It might be helpful if you would come down to the station and look through our mug shots. Maybe she's been arrested before and has a record. If you can pick her out, we can find her."

"Well, of course. When do you want me to come?"

Cole glanced at his watch and then back to her. "When is convenient for you? I know you have the twins to take care of."

"That's no problem," she said. "My assistant, Mandy, is here now, as is Mrs. Green. I also had some more of my security team arrive this morning, so I feel safe leaving them here. It's almost their lunchtime, and then they'll take a nap. I suppose right now is as good a time as any."

Cole pushed to his feet and turned to Dan, who had also risen. "Why don't you and Jason go on? I have my car here. I can bring Holly to the station."

Dan glanced down at his watch. "Okay. Are you going to need me for this?"

"No. Why?"

"I'd asked for the afternoon off. My wife and I had planned to take our grandson to the aquarium over at Gatlinburg. I'll have my cell phone with me in case you need me."

"No problem. Jason can ride back to the station with me. Go on and have a good time. I'll let you know if we learn anything."

"Sounds good," Dan said. "I'll see you tomorrow." He turned to Holly and held out his hand. "It was nice meeting you, Miss Lee. My wife and I are big fans. And we're going to do everything we can to find out who's behind these attempts on your niece and nephew."

Holly smiled and shook his hand. "Thank you, Detective Welch."

Jason closed his sketch pad and grinned at her as he extended his hand. "This has been a real pleasure, Miss Lee."

Holly laughed and shook his hand. "Thank you, Jason. It was nice to meet a fellow musician." He smiled at her, and a thought popped into her head. "Does your band have any performances scheduled around here for the next week or so?"

He nodded. "Yeah. There's a rock festival at the Gatlinburg Convention Center tonight. We're playing in that."

"I would love to hear you play. Maybe I can come."

Cole frowned and shook his head. "I don't think that's a good idea, Holly. You need to stay out of the public eye until we know more about what's up with these threats against the twins."

"You're right, of course," she said. "But isn't there some place I could stand that is isolated from the crowd where I could see the performances?"

His brow wrinkled as he seemed to ponder her words. "I know some of the staff there. Maybe I could get them to let you into the control booth."

"Oh, that would be great! Just let me know what time to be there, and I'll have my team bring me."

He hesitated a moment before he spoke. "I still think this isn't such a good idea."

"Why not?" She could tell he was struggling with something he wanted to say but couldn't bring himself to do it. "Tell me, Cole. What is the problem?"

He frowned and rubbed the back of his neck. "You've been involved in some serious attacks in the last twenty-four hours. Even if you were able to disguise your appearance, arriving at the convention center with an entourage of bodyguards is going to attract attention. You've already drawn enough attention to yourself by going to the supermarket yesterday. I'm surprised there aren't photographers camped all over your front yard."

She thought about what he'd said before she responded. "I think you're right. I won't take my security team. You can take me instead."

"Me?" She struggled to keep from laughing at the shocked look on his face. "I don't remember saying that I wanted to go hear Jason. I've heard his band before, and believe me, my eardrums haven't been the same since."

Jason grinned and elbowed Cole in the ribs. "Come on, man—you're exaggerating. I think Miss Lee has a great idea. You can help her keep a low profile, and she'll get to hear us play."

"Jason's right, Cole," Holly said. "What do you say? Want to be my bodyguard for the night?"

She could tell he wanted to protest, but then he exhaled and shook his head. "Okay, you win. But I'm warning you now—you'd better do everything I tell you to."

Holly clicked her heels together and gave a snappy salute. "Aye, aye, captain. And what time will you pick me up?"

He glanced at Jason. "What time does your band hit the stage?"

"We're the next to the last group to perform," he said.

Cole nodded and looked back at Holly. "The concert starts at seven, so I'll pick you up about then. By the time we get there, the crowd should all be inside, and we can slip in unnoticed."

"That sounds good. I'll expect you."

He inhaled a deep breath. "Now that's settled. So let's get back to the business at hand. Are you ready to go look at those mug shots?"

"I am. Let me go tell Mandy and Mrs. Green where I'll be." She headed to the kitchen and smiled when she pushed the door open and saw Emma and Ethan in their high chairs having their lunch. Mandy sat in front of Emma to assist her while Mrs. Green helped Ethan.

She stood still and let her gaze drift over the babies. She'd had them for three weeks now, and it was amazing how much they had changed in that short time. As she watched, Ethan grabbed for the spoon Mrs. Green was about to shove into his mouth and gave a loud squeal. He'd just let her know that he wanted to do it himself.

Holly laughed to herself as her gaze drifted to Emma. She had strained carrots smeared across her mouth, and she grinned up at Mandy. They were already trying to walk, and it wouldn't be long before they'd be tearing around the house and going in different directions probably. Life would get interesting then.

Emma glanced her way and laughed when she saw Holly at the door. She held up her arms, begging to be picked up. Holly walked over and kissed her on the forehead. "Hi, messy girl," she said. "Looks like you're enjoying your lunch."

Then she stepped over and kissed Ethan before she looked from Mandy to Mrs. Green. "I'm going to the sheriff's department to look at some mug shots. Will the two of you be okay with the children until I get back?"

Mrs. Green smiled and wiped Ethan's mouth. "Don't you worry. We'll take care of these babies."

"Good." Holly started for the door but turned back to Mandy. "Will you let Todd and the team know where I am? Tell them I want security tight on this house until I get back."

"I'll do it," Mandy said as she picked up the sippy cup of milk and handed it to Emma. Holly's heart pricked as she watched Emma bring the cup to her mouth and take a long drink. How Ruth would have wanted to be here to watch her children growing up. The loss of her sister grew more painful with each passing day, and she doubted if the hole in her heart left by Ruth's death would ever heal.

With tears in her eyes, she turned away and headed back to the den, where Cole was waiting. She only hoped this trip to the sheriff's department would prove fruitful. As soon as this threat was resolved, she would be able to focus on selling the ranch. Then she and the twins would be out of Jackson Springs, and she would never have any reason to come back.

She told herself that was what she wanted, but she knew she was only fooling herself. Ruth and Michael might be gone, but Cole would still be here. Through the years, she'd kept up with him through Ruth, but once she was back in Nashville she probably would never see or hear from him again. Now, all she had to do was convince herself that was really what she wanted. It was going to be easier said than done.

At a few minutes before seven o'clock that night, Cole stood on the front porch of Holly's house ready to knock. He paused for a moment and thought back over the afternoon they'd spent together while she looked at mug shots. Unfortunately, she hadn't seen anyone who looked familiar, and he had brought her back home around four o'clock to get ready for the concert.

As he stood there, he thought once again that taking her out tonight was a mistake. Looking at mug shots was one thing but going to a concert was quite another. One was professional while the other might

give the appearance of being social. And he didn't
need that. In fact, when he'd first seen her the night
of the attempted abduction, he'd promised himself
he would stay as far away from her as possible. But
that didn't seem to be working out too well for him.
All he could do now was try to get through the night,
and then it was back to his original plan to keep his
distance.

With that decided, he pushed the doorbell and waited
for someone to answer. When the door opened, a young
woman, who appeared to be in her late twenties or
early thirties, stood there, smiling at him. Her dark
hair brushed her shoulders, and she tucked one side
behind her ear as she stared at him.

"Hi. I'm Mandy. You must be Cole. Holly is just
saying good-night to the children. If you'll follow me,
I'll show you to the den, and you can wait in there
while I go to tell her you're here."

Cole stepped into the foyer and shook his head.
"No need to show me the way. I'm very familiar
with this house."

"Then make yourself at home," she called out as
she headed to the stairs.

Cole walked toward the room that held so many
memories. At the entryway, he paused. Then he took
a deep breath and strode into the den. There had
been other people in here with him earlier today, and
that had made it easy to ignore the way his stomach churned at being in this house again. He'd been
right to be concerned that tonight wouldn't be easy.
He glanced around and tried to concentrate on the
changes Ruth had made in the room when she and
Michael took over the ranch, but it was no use. The

feeling of déjà vu that had settled over him when he walked through the door into the den increased with each passing minute.

It was impossible to count how many times during his teenage years he'd sat in this room waiting for Holly to come down those stairs. The memory of how nervous he'd been as a young boy to be greeted at the door by Holly's father and escorted into this room to be questioned about where they were going, who would be there and what time they'd be home returned, and he smiled.

Back then, he'd resented the third degree he'd had to undergo each time he picked her up; but now, years later, he respected it for what it had been—a loving father making sure that his daughter was protected. He'd liked Holly's father. In fact, he'd liked all of Holly's family and had thought one day he would have a place of his own at their dinner table. But that dream, along with everything else he'd intended for his future, had died when Holly left town.

Now she was back, and for some reason someone had placed her and the twins in danger. If it wasn't for that, he probably wouldn't have known she was in town. She'd visited Ruth through the years, but she had never attempted to contact him. That shouldn't have surprised him, though. Right before she left, he had given her an ultimatum—forget the obsession she had with becoming a country-music star and marry him or go to Nashville knowing that their relationship was over and he would never take her back. She'd chosen the second one, and although it had been hard, he had learned to accept it and had gotten on with his life.

Before he had time to take a longer trip down memory lane, he heard her coming down the stairs and he rose to greet her. When she walked into the room, his breath hitched in his throat at how beautiful she looked tonight. She wore jeans, a denim jacket with a fitted white T-shirt underneath and a pair of cowboy boots that he guessed probably cost a week's salary for him. She had a baseball cap pulled low over her eyes and a pair of sunglasses in her hand. Her skin seemed to glow with its light dusting of makeup, and for a moment, she looked like the young girl he'd known so long ago.

She smiled as she came into the room, then stopped and whirled around in front of him. "I was trying to go for incognito. Do you think I was successful?"

What could he say? He wanted to tell her how beautiful she was, but she was probably used to hearing those words from everyone around her. They would have no meaning coming from him. Instead, he cleared his throat and glanced at his watch.

"You'll do," he said. "We'd better be going. One of the convention center's employees is going to be at the back door to let us in. We don't want to keep him waiting."

A hurt expression flickered in her eyes before she lifted her chin and smiled. "Then let's go."

They didn't speak as they left the house and walked to his car, which was parked in the circle driveway. She glanced up at him as he opened her door and stepped back for her to climb in. The muscle in his jaw clenched, and he wondered if she noticed how ill at ease he was. He didn't have to wait long to find out.

"Okay, Cole. What's wrong? If you don't want to go, I can stay here. I understand."

He exhaled a deep breath and shook his head. "It's fine, Holly. I've just had a rough few days. Get in the car or we're going to be late."

She stared at him for a moment as if deciding what she wanted to do. Then, with a sigh, she climbed in and pulled her seat belt around her. Cole slammed the door and walked around the back of the car but stopped at the trunk. For a moment, he leaned his hand on the car and closed his eyes.

This wasn't good.

He shouldn't be here.

He didn't want to be here.

He should tell her to go back inside and let him go back to the lonely house he called home.

His glance through the rearview window settled on her figure sitting quite still in his car. She looked so small and so fragile, and the droop of her shoulders hinted at rejection. And suddenly he knew that it didn't matter what Holly asked of him. As long as he had breath in his body, he would do whatever it took to make her happy.

He'd done that ten years ago when he'd let her walk away, and nothing had changed. Right now, she wanted to attend a concert, and he intended to keep her safe while they were there.

He straightened his shoulders, walked around the car and climbed in the driver's side. He turned to her and smiled as he cranked the engine. "Are you ready?" he asked.

His stomach clenched as she reached over and squeezed his hand. "Thank you for this, Cole. Usually, I'm surrounded by staff and security people when I try to go out anywhere. I can't tell you what it means for it just to be you and me, together again where we grew up. I'm going to treasure this night."

He stared at her but didn't say anything. Then he gave a slight nod and drove away from the house.

FIVE

Two hours later, Holly didn't know when she'd enjoyed anything as much as she had the concert. The only thing that would have made it better would have been to be on the floor of the convention center. From the control booth where she and Cole sat, high above the last balcony, she had a clear view of the swirling mass of humanity that stood shoulder to shoulder as they sang along with the bands, waved their arms in the air and danced to the rhythms flowing from the stage. At the present time, though, the stagehands were busy tearing down a set and getting ready for Jason's band.

She turned to Cole and noticed that he had a more relaxed look on his face than he'd had when they first arrived. Their careful planning had paid off—no one had seen them arrive, and they were able to ride the service elevator up without being spotted.

She leaned over toward Cole and smiled. "Are you having a good time?"

He returned her smile and nodded. "It's been a long time since I've been to a concert. I'd forgotten how much the crowd gets into the music."

She wondered if he was thinking about the days when he'd played with her in Ilex, and they traveled all over the South, trying to break into the music world. And it had happened one night in Muscle Shoals, Alabama, when a record producer caught their act in a bar and expressed interest in having them send some of their songs to him.

At first, Cole had been all for it, but she realized later it was only because he didn't think it would go anywhere. When the producer had offered them a contract, things changed abruptly. In the end, he dropped out of the band, and she went to Music City to pursue her dream while he stayed behind in Jackson Springs. She'd wanted him to keep his partnership in Ilex, the botanical name for Holly that he'd given the group, but he refused. Their parting had not been a cordial one, and she'd wondered many times over the years since if there was something else she could have done to make him stay in the group. That didn't matter now, though. They both had their lives, and they'd outgrown that closeness they'd once shared.

She sensed movement at the computer-controlled console where Tim, the audio technician, and Ben, the light technician, were working. Glancing over at Ben, Tim said, "Ready to bring the lights up," and Holly directed her attention back to the stage.

The lights slowly lit up the stage to reveal Jason and his band, The Mavericks, poised and ready to play. She leaned forward in her chair and watched as Jason gave the downbeat, and the bass player began a repetitive rhythmic pattern that blared from the stage. The crowd went wild. As Jason and the other members joined the bass, Holly knew from the looks on their faces that they were experiencing the thrill of connecting with their audience. She sat back in her chair and closed her eyes as she let the music speak to her soul. Jason had really found the sound that roots rock had become known for. A sigh of contentment escaped her lips as she opened her eyes and turned to Cole. His eyes were locked on the stage.

Then he turned to her and smiled. "He's really nailed it, hasn't he? He's got the twelve bar forty-eight beat structure, and those syncopated rhythms are off the charts. I can't believe the way he's flattened those notes and combined them with breakdowns from bluegrass. I think I have underestimated the boy."

With that said, he directed his attention back to the stage, but Holly couldn't take her eyes off him. When he had tried to convince her to stay, he'd told her that he didn't care anything about music, that he'd only gone along with the band idea because she'd wanted it. But she'd known even then that he was lying—to himself if not to her. Music used to light him up. Apparently, it still did. The rapt attention he was giving the performance told her that he still had the love that filled you with the greatest joy when performing. So why had he been so willing to give it up? Even years later, she still didn't understand. After a few minutes, she shook her head and directed her attention back to Jason and his band. She supposed she would never have the answer to that question.

There was only one group left to perform after The Mavericks, but Holly and Cole had decided they would leave before the concert ended in hopes of getting away from the building before anyone saw them. As soon as Jason left the stage, Cole leaned over. "Are you ready to go?"

She nodded, grabbed her jacket that she'd taken off earlier and pulled the cap back down on her head. "Yes. Let's go."

She shook hands with Tim and Ben and thanked them for letting her and Cole sit with them. Then they were out the door and headed to the elevator. Holly was glad that this floor was closed to concertgoers, as they reached the doors without seeing anyone. Once on the ground floor, they walked toward the exit where Cole had parked the car.

The minute they stepped outside the building, a swarm of people converged from out of nowhere and surrounded them. She gasped in shock as her gaze darted over the group. Some she could tell were reporters due to their cameras with telescopic lenses. Others appeared to be attendees armed with cell phones in video mode, and they were recording every move she made. By morning, she and Cole would be pasted all over social media. But worst of all were the questions reporters were screaming at her.

"Is it true that there have been two attempts to kidnap your niece and nephew since you've been in Jackson Springs?"

"Have you increased your security because of these threats?"

"Has this changed your plans for your scheduled tour?"

She wanted to cover her ears, close her eyes and wait for the noise and chaos and badgering to just go away…but years of experience had taught her better.

She couldn't bring herself to respond to the insensitive questioning that hit her right where her heart was most vulnerable, but she could—and did—keep her head up and her expression fixed and calm as she looked for any opening through the converging crowd.

Suddenly Cole's voice roared above all the noise. "Get away from her!"

He wrapped his arm around her and shoved a reporter out of their way as he tried to make a path to the car. "Get out of our way," he snarled as he guided her through the crowd.

She relaxed against him and let him pull her forward until they reached the car. Then he jerked the door open, pushed her inside and closed it. Before she had her seat belt on, he was in the driver's seat, and they were pulling onto the street that ran in front of the convention center. Once they were safely away from the clamor that had surrounded them, she exhaled and straightened. "Thank you, Cole, for helping me back there."

He glanced in the rearview mirror, checking to see if they were being followed, and shook his head. "I'm sorry you had to go through that, Holly. Someone must have leaked the word that you'd be there tonight."

"It's not your fault. I'm just thankful you were with me." She was quiet for a minute before she spoke again. "I shouldn't have gone."

He glanced over at her, a surprised expression on his face. "I thought you had a good time."

"I did while I was there, and I'm glad I got to hear Jason's band play. They're really good."

Cole chuckled. "Yeah, they are. I know they have quite a following in this area, but I've kidded him about how it hurts my ears. It's different from the country music we used to make."

"Yeah," she said. "It sure is." A tear formed in the corner of her eye and trickled down the side of her face.

"I just wanted to be normal for one night."

He jerked his head around and stared at her. "What do you mean?"

She swallowed the lump that had formed in her throat before she spoke. "Don't get me wrong. I'm grateful for how God has blessed me with my music, but sometimes I wish I had my old life back."

"Holly, I…" He stopped as if he didn't know how to finish his sentence.

She reached over and squeezed his arm. "It's okay. It's just that every time I go out, there are people there snapping my picture and yelling questions at me. I just want to go to a restaurant or a movie and blend in with the crowd. I don't want to be singled out all the time. Does that make sense?"

He nodded. "Perfectly. That must be very hard on you."

A sudden thought hit her, and she squeezed his arm tighter. "Is that why you didn't come with me? Because you didn't want to take a chance that success would take over your life?"

He didn't take his eyes off the road as they drove through the night toward her house. He gripped the steering wheel harder, and his teeth clenched. "That's part of it, I guess. But I knew I didn't have the drive to succeed like you did. I didn't want to be there when you figured out that I was just dead weight you were having to carry around."

His words shocked her, and she gasped. "Cole, I would never have thought that. I loved you."

"And I loved you, too. I thought you deserved better than a guy whose big ambition had always been to become a cop."

"Cole, please don't say…"

"I came after you, you know."

His words washed over her like she'd just been hit with a bucket of ice water, and she turned to stare at him. "What did you say?"

He didn't look at her as he spoke. "About a year after you left, I couldn't stand being parted from you any longer, and I came to Nashville to find you. I wanted to tell you I'd do anything if you'd give me one more chance."

"B-but I never saw you."

"I saw you, though," he said. "You were performing at a little bar down on Broadway close to Ryman Auditorium, and I stood in the back of the room and watched you. I saw how the crowd connected with you and how you were right where you needed to be. I knew that night you were right on the verge of making it big, and I decided I'd been right to let you go. So I turned around and walked out."

Another tear ran down her cheek, and she wiped it away. "Oh, Cole, things might have been so different if I'd known you were there."

He chuckled and shook his head. "No. Everything worked out just the way it was supposed to."

She started to protest, but he turned into the driveway of her house. He pulled to a stop, came around the car and opened her door. When he took her arm and guided her up the front steps, she knew their conversation had ended. Todd stood on the front porch with his arms crossed in front of him.

"Good evening, Miss Lee. Detective Jackson," he said.

"Hello, Todd," she said. "How have things been around here tonight?"

"Very quiet. Did you have a good time?"

She sighed. "Up until we ran into a swarm of reporters. Somehow, they've gotten wind of the attempts on the twins, so I imagine they'll be camped on our front yard by morning."

"We'll be prepared for them, ma'am."

She smiled and turned back to Cole. "Thank you again for taking me tonight. I had a really good time."

"I enjoyed it, too." He turned to leave but suddenly froze and walked over to where she stood. "On second thought, why don't we all go inside for a few minutes?"

The tone of his voice sent chills down her spine. "What's the matter, Cole?"

"Inside. Now, Holly," he ordered as he raised his eyebrows at Todd.

She opened the door, and the three of them filed into the entryway. Once inside, Cole shut the door and turned back to them. "I saw movement in the trees to the right of the house. It could have been an animal, but it looked too big. Todd, you stay here with Holly. I'll go out the back door and circle around to see if there's somebody out there watching the house."

Holly's heart pounded, and she reached out for Cole. "Be careful."

"I will be." He glanced at Todd. "Are any of your men out back?"

"Ray's on the back porch. I'll text him and tell him you're coming by."

"Cole…" she said, but it was too late. He was already striding toward the rear of the house.

Ray raised his hand in greeting but didn't say anything as Cole prowled past him and out into the dark night. Evidently, he had gotten the message. Cole gave a slight nod and eased out into the shadows that covered the backyard.

The tree line of a forest that started next to the property and spread up the mountain sat to the right of the house, and Cole crept to it. A cloud covering the moon had blocked out what little light he'd had before. Now all he could see was the black void beyond the trees. Maybe he'd only thought he saw movement. It could have been a tree branch blowing in the breeze.

He stopped and listened for anything that seemed out of place. At first, he heard nothing, but then the snap of a twig jerked his attention to the right of where he stood. He pulled his gun from the shoulder holster and eased forward.

With his gun clutched in his hand and his finger on the trigger, he inched closer to the spot where he thought the sound had come from. He'd only gone a few feet when he spotted the outline of a figure hunched behind a tree. From where he stood, he couldn't tell if the person had a weapon or not, and he braced himself for what he was about to encounter.

He crept a few steps farther and then circled to the right so that he was close enough to see the back of the person standing behind the tree. The moon emerged from the cloud where it had been hiding and cast a faint glow to the forest below. In the dim light, he could make out the figure a little better. As he watched, the body shifted so that one hand rested on the tree trunk and his head tilted up as he stared at the house.

Cole followed the intruder's gaze to the window in a lit room on the second floor. As he watched, he saw Mandy, Holly's assistant, come into view as she walked past. As she did, she laughed and looked down at Ethan, who was nestled in her arms. It was only a glimpse, but he knew that brief look had triggered something in the person in front of him. He heard a slight groan, and then the person's body sagged against the tree.

Gripping his gun tighter, Cole stepped forward. "Turn around slowly, and don't try anything stupid!"

He was prepared for the man to turn and fire a gun of his own or charge at him in anger, but he wasn't prepared for the sound of the hysterical crying that greeted his command. What rocked him even more was the frightened feminine voice that answered him. "P-please, m-mister, don't kill me. I won't tell anybody if you'll just let me go. I promise to leave and never come back."

Frowning at the strange words the woman spoke, Cole eased closer. "Nobody's going to kill you. I'm

Detective Cole Jackson. Who are you, and what are you doing outside Holly Lee's house?"

The woman's crying stopped immediately, and she gave a relieved sigh. "Oh, Detective Jackson. I'm so glad it's you. I thought he'd found me. He said he would, and he said he would kill me."

Cole eased toward the woman but stopped when he was close enough to make out the woman's features. Right away, he recognized her. She was the woman Holly had described to Jason, the one who'd been watching her at the supermarket. On top of that, something about her voice sounded familiar, and he wondered if she could be the woman who'd called him, the one he'd gone to Sturgis Road Mall to find.

"Did you call me yesterday at the station?"

She nodded and sniffed. "Yes, sir. I had to end the call in a hurry because he'd seen me, and I had to get away. So I ran into the supermarket."

"You were watching Holly Lee inside that store, and now tonight I find you outside her home. What's this all about? Why are you stalking Holly, and what do you mean someone's trying to kill you?"

"I'm not stalking her. I just want to talk to her."

"You want to talk to her about what?"

She shook her head. "I need to tell Miss Lee. Will you let me talk to her?"

"Look, Miss…" He paused. "What is your name?"

"Sarah Palmer."

Cole slipped his gun back in its holster. "Well then, Miss Palmer. Suppose you tell me what's so important that you have people trying to kill you and you need to talk to Holly."

"I'll tell you, but I have to tell her, too."

He shook his head. "Tell me first, and I'll decide if it's important enough for us to involve Holly."

"Oh, it's important enough. Believe me."

Cole snorted in disgust. "Don't be so dramatic. Just tell me, and we'll go from there."

Sarah crossed her arms over her chest and shook her head. "No."

He stared at the determined look on her face, and he knew from her body language that he was fighting a losing battle. After a moment, he exhaled. "Okay, but I'm going to be right beside you. If you make a move to hurt Holly, I'll stop you and arrest you on the spot."

"That's fine with me. Just give me the chance to talk with her."

Cole let his gaze drift over her before he let it settle on her face. "I need to make sure you don't have any hidden weapons before we go inside. Take off your jacket and hand it to me."

She did as he asked and then held her arms straight out to her sides. She wore a pair of tight-fitting jeans and a fitted T-shirt. He could tell at first glance she'd have to be a magician to hide a weapon in those clothes. There wasn't a gun or a knife in the jacket, but he decided to hold on to it until after they'd had their talk with Holly.

"Okay," he said, "let's go. But remember, I'll be watching you."

She didn't say anything as he led her back to the house and up to the front door. When they entered, Holly and Todd rushed out of the den but came to a halt when they saw the woman accompanying him.

Holly gasped and put her hand to her throat. "You're the woman I saw at the supermarket yesterday."

Sarah nodded. "Yes."

Holly turned a questioning glance to Cole, and he shrugged. "Holly, this is Sarah Palmer. She says she needs to talk to you, and she'll only tell me why she's been following you if you are present when she does."

A small frown wrinkled Holly's brow, and she looked from Cole to Sarah. "Okay," she said. "I'm listening. What do you want to tell me?"

Sarah's throat constricted as she swallowed before speaking. "I've practiced this so many times, but I didn't really think I'd ever get the chance to tell you."

Holly tilted her head to one side and frowned. "I'd never seen you before until yesterday, and I have no idea what connection you think you have to me, but you need to tell me now."

Sarah took a deep breath before she cut her eyes to Cole and then back to Holly. "The airplane crash that killed your sister and brother-in-law wasn't an accident. They were murdered."

SIX

Of all the things Sarah could have said, that was the last thing Holly would have expected. Her statement was so shocking that Holly could only stare at her in stunned silence. Then she shook her head and narrowed her eyes. "Why are you doing this? How could you come into my house and make a statement like that? Are you on drugs or something?"

"I'm telling the truth. Your brother-in-law was given a drug in a cup of coffee right before the plane took off, and they went down when he lost consciousness."

Holly glanced at Cole, who looked as shocked as she felt. "Sarah," he said, "that's a serious allegation. What possessed you to come here and make such a claim?"

"The fact that I know it's true," she said.

At that statement, Todd, who'd stood quietly by Holly since Cole brought Sarah in, stepped in front of Sarah. "I think it's time you left. If you won't go peacefully, I'm going to remove you bodily from this house."

Before Cole could tell Todd he wanted to question

Sarah further, the bodyguard took another step forward. He reached out to take Sarah by the arm, but she jerked away. "You've got to believe me! I risked my life to come here and tell you!" Sarah screamed.

A worried look crossed Todd's face, and Holly could tell that he thought Sarah was mentally disturbed and possibly dangerous. "That does it," he said. "You're out of here."

Cole held out his hand to stop him. "Wait, Todd. This is a serious allegation, and we need to get to the bottom of this. If this is true, the authorities need to be involved."

Todd hesitated, but then he backed off. "You're right."

Cole turned back to Sarah. "You need to get yourself under control, and we'll sit down and talk so you can tell us why you think Ruth and Michael were murdered." He glanced at Todd. "Show Sarah into the den, and Holly and I will be there shortly."

Todd nodded and motioned for Sarah to follow him. When they were out of earshot, Holly blinked back tears and turned to Cole. "Do you think she's telling the truth? Why would anybody want to kill Ruth and Michael? They didn't have an enemy in the world."

"I know this is upsetting, Holly," he said, "but we need to find out why she's making this accusation. After we've heard her out, I'll know better what I need to do. Does she really know something about a murder, or is she in need of psychiatric attention? Let's go listen to what she has to say. Okay?"

Holly bit down on her lip and thought about what he'd said. She'd known some crazy fans over the years, but she'd never encountered anything like this. There were people who stalked celebrities and concocted all kinds of stories to get the attention of the person they were fixated on. Just another downside to living in the public eye. Sarah could easily be one of them. It was at times like these that she wished she'd never left Jackson Springs.

But this was a serious situation, and it needed to be settled right away. Cole was right. He could better decide how to handle this situation after he heard Sarah's story. She took a deep breath and nodded. "Okay. Let's go see what she has to say."

When they walked into the den, Sarah was seated on the sofa and Todd was standing beside her as if he was afraid she might bolt at any minute. Holly took a seat in a chair facing Sarah, and Cole eased down beside her on the couch. Todd stepped over beside Holly and took a protective stance next to her.

Cole glanced at Holly before he swiveled to face Sarah. "I hope you can understand how your statement has upset Miss Lee. She's still grieving the loss of her sister and brother-in-law while making a life for their two orphaned children. I have to warn you, if this is some wild scheme to benefit you in some way, whether it's to extort money from her or to gain you fifteen minutes of fame, I will personally see that you pay to the full extent of the law."

Sarah clasped her hands in her lap and nodded. "I understand. This isn't easy for me. In fact, I kept trying to talk myself out of coming here." She paused and looked at Holly. "But a few days ago, I saw some pictures of you in a magazine at Malibu. You had your niece and nephew with you, and the story said you'd taken them after their parents died. When I saw those two children, I knew I had to come forward with what I know."

"I remember that article," Holly said. She closed her eyes as the memory of that day washed over her, and she recalled how angry she'd been when that article came out. She and Mandy had waded into the ocean that afternoon and held Emma and Ethan as their tiny hands slapped at the water while the waves rolled in. They had sounded so happy, and their giggles had lifted her spirits for the first time since the tragedy.

She still hadn't figured out how the photographer had gotten past her security guards to take the pictures, but they had.

"Well," Sarah said, "after I saw those pictures, I wrestled with what I should do. And then I decided that no matter what happened to me, I had to let you know."

Before she could say anything else, Cole leaned toward her, a frown on his face. "Okay, Sarah. I want you to start at the beginning and tell us what brought you to the conclusion that Ruth and Michael were murdered."

Sarah nodded and took a deep breath. "I suppose the beginning came about a year and a half ago when I met a man at the restaurant where I worked as a waitress. He came in one night and he flirted with me the whole time he was there. I was shocked when I saw the tip he'd left but thought I'd probably never see him again. But he was back the next night and asked me to go out with him. I don't usually date men I don't know well, but he was insistent. He came in night after night until I gave in. To my surprise, he was very charming and very attentive. I liked him right away, and we began to see each other."

Cole had pulled his notepad from his pocket and was busy scribbling notes of what Sarah was saying. When she paused, he glanced up. "What was his name?"

"Willie Trask. He was a sharp dresser and always had a lot of money, so he showed me a good time when we went out."

"Where did he work?" Cole asked.

"That's the strange part," Sarah answered. "He would never give me a straight answer about his job but told me he consulted with businesses on problems and did troubleshooting for them. He would leave town and be gone for days. Then he'd return, and he'd take me out to a fancy restaurant to celebrate his success with another assignment, but he'd never tell me where he went or who he helped."

A frown pulled at Cole's brow. "Didn't you get suspicious about what he was doing?"

"Not at first, but then things changed."

"What happened?"

"Willie had been out of town for a few days on business in Dallas, he said. When he came home, we decided to have dinner at his apartment that night. Before we ate, I needed to go freshen up. In the bathroom, I saw a book of matches on the floor next to the clothes hamper. I figured it had fallen out of his pocket when he had taken off his dirty clothes. I picked it up and was surprised to see that it was from a motel in New Orleans. When I asked him what he was doing in New Orleans, he got angry and told me

I had no right snooping around his apartment. For the first time, I saw a side of his personality that frightened me, and I left soon after we ate."

"So he wouldn't tell you anything about where the matchbook came from?"

She shook her head. "No, but I called the motel, and I could tell from talking with whomever answered that it wasn't a very upscale place. In fact, it sounded like a cash-only establishment that rented rooms by the hour. I couldn't imagine what Willie was doing staying in such a place."

"Did you ask him about it again?" Cole asked.

"No. I was going to, but I didn't get a chance. We weren't supposed to see each other the next night, but I decided I had to know more about who he really was. So I went to his apartment. When I got there, I knocked, but he didn't answer. I was surprised that the door wasn't locked, so I walked in. I could hear him on the phone in the bedroom, and I walked over and stopped at the door."

"Who was he talking to?"

"I don't know, but what he said scared me so bad that my knees were wobbling. I heard him say, 'I put the drug in the guy's coffee, and the plane went down. I made the hit just like you wanted. I'll do another one for you if you need me, but I try to stay away from high-profile jobs. And kidnapping a country-music star's kids is high profile. Why do you need these babies?'"

Holly's heart was pounding so hard she felt like it might burst out of her chest. She looked at Cole and opened her mouth to speak, but he shook his head. "Go on, Sarah."

"I couldn't move, and he didn't say anything for a few minutes while he listened to whoever he was talking to. Then I heard him say, 'How much are they willing to pay?' He gave a low chuckle and said, 'Not much for the coverage this is going to get in the media when a celebrity is involved. Instead, I want half of the payoff if I get those kids for you. Take it or leave it.' He listened for a few more minutes then said, 'I thought you'd see it my way. I'll be in touch.' Before I could move, he disconnected the call and turned around. That's when he saw me, and I knew from the rage on his face I had to get out of there. I ran as fast as I could, but I could hear him shouting at me that he was going to kill me."

"What did you do then?" Cole asked.

"I drove to the ATM, got some money and took off for a fishing cabin that my father had on the lake. I'd never told Willie about it, so I thought I'd be safe there. The next day, I went to the library in a nearby town and searched the internet for stories that involved a plane crash, children and a country-music star. I found the story about your sister and brother-in-law crashing in Louisiana, and I knew he'd killed them. I've been trying to get my nerve up ever since to come here. But I waited too long, because now he knows where I am." She glanced at Cole. "That's why I called you. Because I saw him on the street in town, and I knew it had something to do with what I'd heard him saying on the phone. But then he saw me, and the look on his face told me he wanted to make good on his threat to kill me to keep me quiet."

Holly watched Cole's face to see if she could tell whether he believed Sarah or not, but there was nothing visible to give a hint as to what he was thinking. He stared down at his notes for a moment and then sighed before looking up. "That's a good story, Sarah. But we all know that the reports of Ruth's and Michael's deaths and their orphaned children have been in the news a lot since their deaths. It might not have been that way if it wasn't for Holly's celebrity, but it's been reported widely. Anybody could take those facts and make up a story that sounded like it was true. Have you been truthful with us, or are you lying?"

Tears rolled down her cheeks, and she shook her head. "I'm not lying. That's exactly what happened. You've got to believe me. I couldn't live with myself if something happened to those children and I hadn't come forward."

Cole pursed his lips and stared back down at his notes. Then he glanced up at Todd. "Would you stay here with Sarah while Holly and I have a private conversation?"

Todd nodded, and Holly stood and followed Cole from the room. He led her to the kitchen, where he closed the door before he turned to face her. "Holly, I don't know for sure, but I tend to believe her. She appeared so emotional when she was talking. This raises some suspicions that we need to check out."

Holly sank down in a chair at the kitchen table, propped her elbows on the tabletop and covered her eyes. With the first words out of Sarah's mouth, she had known she was about to hear something that would affect her greatly. But she hadn't expected it to turn her world upside down. Ruth and Michael murdered, and someone being paid to kidnap Ethan and Emma? It seemed too surreal to be true.

She sensed that Cole had pulled a chair close to her and sat beside her. "Holly, are you all right?"

She shook her head. "I don't think I ever will be again." She blinked back her tears and looked up into his face. "What are we going to do, Cole?"

He reached over and took her hand in his. "We're going to find out the truth. If this Willie Trask actually exists, I'm going to find him and find out who's paying him so I can put a stop to his plan before he does any more harm to you or your family."

She stared into his eyes and then down at their hands. A small smile curled her lips. "Did you hear what we said, Cole? I asked what *we* were going to do, and you said *we* were going to find out the truth. It sounds almost like old times when we worked everything out together."

A sad look flashed in his eyes, and he nodded. "It's always been that way, and no matter what's happened between us in the past, it still is. We're going to get to the bottom of this and protect Ethan and Emma while we're doing it."

"How are we going to do that?"

"I have a few ideas. Now I need to make some phone calls. You go back in the den, and I'll be there in a few minutes."

As they stood, their eyes locked, and Holly felt a flutter in her stomach that she hadn't felt in years. The thought that all she wanted was to press her lips to his consumed her, but she knew it was years too late for that. Reluctantly, she stepped back, breaking their contact.

"I'll be with Todd," she murmured before heading to the door.

She didn't look back as she walked away but focused on holding her emotions in check before she fell to pieces. When she stepped back in the den, Sarah still sat on the couch, and Todd stood beside her. She gave a slight nod and sat down in the chair she'd vacated earlier.

No one spoke as they waited for Cole to reappear. After what seemed to be an interminable time, he walked back in. He came and sat on the sofa next to Sarah again. "I've talked with the sheriff and with social services. We think it's best if we place you in a safe house for the time being. We can protect you there while we dig into what you've told us."

She nodded. "Okay. Can we go by the motel where I'm staying and get my stuff?"

He shook his head. "I don't think that's such a good idea. There will be clothes and all kinds of personal items for your use where you're going. If someone really is trying to kill you, they may have your motel staked out. One of the deputies can clean the room out later, but we don't want to lead them to the safe house."

"How long do you think I'll have to stay there?"

Cole shrugged. "I can't promise how long you'll be there."

Sarah sank back against the cushions of the sofa and sighed. "Thank you. I feel safe for the first time in weeks. I hope you hurry up and find him so I can go home. I need to get back to my job—that is, if I still have one."

"Maybe it won't take long." With that, he stood and Sarah joined him.

Holly wanted to follow them to the door, but her

knees felt weak. "Todd, will you show Detective Jackson and Miss Palmer out?"

Cole cocked an eyebrow and cast a questioning glance at her. "Holly, I'll come by in the morning."

She didn't answer him, and after a minute, he and Todd escorted Sarah outside. The front door closed and Todd walked back to the den. "I'm going to make a call to that security company in Knoxville we've used before and get them to send some of their guys to help us out tonight so we can double our guard. Mandy is upstairs with the babies. Why don't you go on up and try to get a good night's sleep? We'll make sure that all of you are protected."

"Thanks, Todd. I just want to sit here for a while and think about everything that's happened tonight. But don't let me detain you. Go on and do whatever you need to."

He didn't say anything else but slipped from the room. As the hour grew later, she couldn't make herself get up and go to bed. All she could think about was what Sarah had said. Losing Ruth in such a horrific way had been unbearable, but if Sarah was telling the truth, she doubted if she would ever recover from the fact that someone had planned and executed her sister's death in such a methodical and diabolical way. Holly doubted if she would ever recover from the gaping wound left by such a hideous act.

The next morning, Cole could hardly wait to get back to Holly's house and see how she'd made it through the night. After getting past the paparazzi parked in front of the house and one of the new security guards he hadn't seen before, he strode through the front door and to the kitchen, where all the morning sounds were coming from.

Emma and Ethan were in their high chairs and Holly and Mandy were laughing as they tried to feed the twins their morning cereal. Mrs. Green stood at the stove, her hands on her hips and a smile on her face. To see Holly as happy as she appeared to be at that moment warmed his heart. He'd been worried she'd be down in the dumps after what she'd heard the night before.

He watched for a few minutes before he cleared his throat. "Is this a private party, or can anybody get in on it?"

Holly looked up and smiled when she saw him. "I'm afraid Mandy and I are busy right now, but if you want cereal, I'm sure Mrs. Green would be glad to feed you."

He laughed and pulled out a chair from the table. "You always did have a smart mouth," he teased as he sat down.

She gazed up at him from hooded eyes. "I learned it from you. I had to if I was going to hold my own with you."

Mandy paused before sticking the spoon in Emma's mouth. "Oh, I forgot. You two grew up together." She grinned at Cole. "Tell me, Detective, what was my boss like as a little girl? Was she as determined to do everything by the book as she is now?"

Cole threw back his head and laughed. "Not by a long shot. She was the kid who was always getting in trouble at school. Everybody knew not to mess with her, because they didn't want to bring Holly's Folly down on their heads."

Holly's face turned crimson. "Hush. You're going to make Mandy and Mrs. Green think I was a monster child."

He shrugged. "Well, all I'm saying is that the school's still trying to find out who put the snake in Debbie Taylor's desk. When it came slithering out, she screamed and turned over in her chair, then crawled across the floor in a panic, trying to get away from it. It took the teacher the rest of the morning to calm the class down."

Holly reached over and swatted him on the arm. "Oh, you're making it sound so much worse than it was. Besides, it was just a little garter snake that wouldn't hurt a soul." She grinned and paused for effect. "Or at least that's what I heard."

Cole arched his eyebrows, and Mandy burst out laughing. "It sounds like the two of you had a wonderful childhood."

Cole's eyes softened as he stared at Holly. "The best in the world. I wouldn't trade my memories for anything."

Holly set the empty cereal bowl on the table and reached over and wiped Ethan's mouth. "I hate to put a damper on this trip down memory lane, but did you want to see me about something, Cole?"

Her words reminded him that no matter what was in the past, this was now, and they had more serious things to discuss. "Oh, yeah. I stopped by to bring you up to date on the attempts on the twins. Do you have time to talk?"

She pushed to her feet and nodded. "Sure. Mrs. Green, would you take over with Ethan while I go with Cole?"

He gritted his teeth and shook his head as Holly walked out of the kitchen with him right behind. It hadn't taken him long to ruin her good mood. He didn't know if it was the talk about their childhood or the investigation that had done it. No matter which it was, from now on he'd have to watch what he said.

When they entered the den, she closed the door and turned to face him. "Did you get Sarah settled last night?"

"Yes. I checked with the counselor who runs the safe house this morning, and she said Sarah had a good night. She's going to talk with her today and see if she can find out anything else from her."

Holly walked over and sat down on the sofa. "So, what's the next move? How are you going to check out her story?"

"I've got people from the sheriff's department checking into the identity of Willie Trask," he explained as he sat down beside her. "It's probably a false name, but if he's been using it long enough, then it might lead to some clues as to crimes he might have committed over the past few years. Sarah will be meeting with a sketch artist later to give a description, so we can see if it matches anyone in our databases. But as for me, I want to follow up on something that's been bothering me since Sarah gave us her story last night."

"What's that?"

"Why is the person behind this so focused on Ethan and Emma? As sad as it is to say, there are plenty of babies out there in the world that are very vulnerable—kids who could be kidnapped without anyone putting up much of a fuss. Why would someone go to these lengths, killing Ruth and Michael and attacking a celebrity, just to get these two particular kids? It got me wondering—is there something about their background that we don't know?"

Holly looked startled, and he waited a moment to let her process. "You could be right," she admitted.

"I was thinking it might be a good idea to talk with the agency that Ruth and Michael used for the adoption. Do you know who it was?"

"Ruth never wanted to talk about it much. She did tell me one time that it was a private adoption that had been arranged through their lawyer, Julie Swanson. She's the one who handled the will and has helped me with settling all their affairs. Do you know her?"

Cole nodded. "I don't know her personally, but I've seen her a few times in court. She's had a practice in Jackson Springs for several years now. From what I've heard, she stays busy. Maybe that's a good place to start. I'll go see her today."

"I'm coming with you," Holly said.

His eyebrows arched in surprise. "Oh, no, you're not. You're going to stay here, where you're safe," he answered. "Besides, there are reporters everywhere outside. If you want to avoid them, you'll stay here."

She shook her head. "I have a car at the back door, and there's a ranch road that leads through the property to the highway at the rear of our land. We can go out that way."

Cole shook his head. "I don't know, Holly…"

Before he could finish, she interrupted him. "I can't let those reporters stop me. If what Sarah said is true, I'm not the one in danger. It's Ethan and Emma who are being targeted. And they'll continue to be until we can find out if Ruth and Michael were really murdered— and put the person responsible behind bars. Now, you can let me come with you, or I'll go alone."

He stared at her and then shook his head. "You're just as stubborn as you were when we were growing up."

She smiled, stood up and stared down at him. "One of my best qualities that's served me well in life."

"And still a thorn in my flesh," he grumbled as he pushed to his feet.

Holly laughed, and the sound sent a warm rush through him. "You wouldn't have it any other way," she said as she headed for the door.

And in that moment, Cole knew she was right. It didn't matter how long she'd been gone or how they'd parted. She had a hold on his heart that he would never be able to shake. And if he was honest with himself, he really wasn't sure how he felt about that.

SEVEN

An hour later, Holly and Cole walked into Julie Swanson's office. Holly had talked with Julie several times over the phone, but her lawyers in Nashville had handled most of the communication that had occurred since the plane crash. She'd never met the lawyer in person. As they came in the door, a receptionist looked up from the computer that sat on her mahogany desk and smiled at them.

"May I help you?"

Cole flipped his wallet open to reveal his badge. "I'm Detective Cole Jackson. I called earlier about speaking to Ms. Swanson."

The woman smiled. "Oh, yes. If you'll have a seat, I'll let her know you're here."

They walked over to a leather couch that sat against a wall with a display of several large framed photographs. Holly leaned closer and studied the pictures of scenes from around the world. In one, a lion peered at the camera from his resting place underneath an acacia tree on an African savanna. Another displayed the towering peak of Mount Everest, and the third showed a Chinese man standing at the oar of a sampan in a crowded harbor.

Holly turned back to the receptionist. "These are beautiful."

She smiled and nodded. "Julie took all of them. She has traveled all over the world, and her home is filled with more photographs."

Holly sat down next to Cole, and he leaned over and whispered in her ear. "I had no idea lawyers in Jackson Springs made enough money to travel extensively abroad. I think I chose the wrong profession."

Holly giggled and poked him in the ribs. "Shh! They'll hear you."

Before he could respond, the receptionist rose to her feet and spoke up. "Julie will see you now. Come this way, please."

They followed her down a narrow hallway to a door at the end. The receptionist tapped lightly before pushing it open. "Go on in."

Since Holly had never seen Julie Swanson before, she had no idea what she looked like. She had expected to see a middle-aged woman who had been practicing law a long time, but instead they were greeted by a thirtysomething woman who could have passed for a model.

Holly had been around high fashion enough for red-carpet events to recognize that Julie was wearing a designer suit. Diamond studs sparkled at her ears, and her perfectly coiffed hair gave the appearance that she might have just stepped off the page of a fashion magazine.

Smiling, she came around the desk and held out her hand. "Detective Jackson, I've heard a lot of good things about you, but I don't think I've had the pleasure of meeting you before." She shook his hand and then turned to Holly. "And, Miss Lee, I've talked with you before, but I've never had the opportunity to tell you in person how sorry I am about Ruth's and Michael's deaths. They had been clients of mine ever since I opened my practice, and I still mourn them deeply."

Holly shook the woman's hand and smiled. "Thank you, Ms. Swanson."

She waved her hand in dismissal. "Now, let's have none of that Ms. Swanson stuff. I'm Julie."

"And I'm Holly," she responded.

Julie's eyes darkened, and Holly saw the sadness there. "How are the children? Are you adjusting to having two one-year-olds to care for?"

"I have to admit I have my days when I don't know if I'll make it or not, but I wouldn't trade places with anyone else."

"Just keep in mind what I told you when we first talked. If the stress of your busy life is too much to allow you to keep the twins, I can assist you with finding suitable adoptive parents for them."

Holly shook her head. "I thought about it at first, but after having them with me, I know I couldn't live without them."

Julie smiled. "I just felt like I should give you all the options, but I have to say I'm glad you chose to keep them. Ruth would be so happy." Julie motioned to the chairs in front of her desk. "Have a seat and tell me what I can do for you today." Seating herself, she folded her hands on top of the desk. "My receptionist said it had something to do with the twins' adoption. Is there a problem?"

Holly glanced at Cole, and he leaned forward. "There's no problem as far as Holly's concerned about the twins, but there is something troubling. There have been two attempts to harm Ethan and Emma in the last few days, and we're trying to get to the bottom of it."

Julie's eyes grew big. "What kind of harm?"

She listened as Cole told her about the break-in and the supermarket experience. When he finished, Julie shook her head in disbelief. "Do you have any suspects?"

"We have a lead we're following about a person of interest, but we haven't been able to find him yet. We need some information about the adoption itself. Holly said you handled it for Ruth and Michael and that it was a private one."

Julie nodded. "Yes. They came to me to see if I could help them. Ruth was at her wits' end with all the in vitro procedures, and the waiting lists at the state-funded adoption centers were too long. They thought I might know someone who could help."

"And did you?" Cole asked.

"Yes. I had heard of a maternity home called Wings of Hope that's about twenty miles from here. They're a facility for women who are pregnant and need care while they're trying to figure out their options. Most of the women are unmarried and are concerned about how they can raise a child on their own. The home offers counseling along with medical care while they're there. Some choose to keep their babies while others put them up for adoption.

But sometimes there's a mother who wants to have a say in who adopts her child. She wants to meet the couple and approve them before she terminates her rights. I contacted the facility and asked if they had anyone at that time who might be interested in a private adoption. They said they had one mother who might."

"And how did you proceed after that?" Cole asked.

"I gave Ruth and Michael the information, and they went to see the girl. From what Michael later told me, they visited her quite a few times so that she could get to know them. The young woman's boyfriend was a soldier who was killed in the Middle East, and neither she nor he had any family. There was no one to help her with the baby. When she found out she was having twins, she knew there was no way she could provide for them on her own. She decided she wanted Ruth and Michael to adopt the babies."

Holly glanced at Cole. "I don't understand why Ruth never told me any of this."

"I don't know the answer to that," Julie said. "All I did was handle the legal work. The mother terminated her rights before the babies were born and granted Michael and Ruth the opportunity to adopt them. They completed a home study through the Department of Children Services and had all the legal papers signed well before the mother went into labor. When the babies were born, Ruth and Michael were able to bring them home from the hospital. All that was left for us to do was go to court for the final adoption."

"What about the mother?" Cole asked.

Julie sighed and rubbed her eyes. "I was told later

that she went back to Wings of Hope to recuperate after leaving the hospital. While she was there, she suffered a blood clot to the heart and died."

Holly's eyes filled with tears. "Oh, how tragic."

Julie nodded. "Yes, it was. I was so happy that we had everything taken care of before she passed away."

Cole sat there for a minute as if he was thinking what to ask next. What he finally said shocked Holly. "Julie, did Michael pay the mother any money to get her to let them adopt the children?"

She shook her head. "No, absolutely not. I told him he could pay for the medical bills for the mother and the twins, but he could not give her any other money."

"Could he have done it without your knowing about it?"

"I suppose so," she said, "but Michael understood that the law specifically states that the adoptive parents can't give the mother any kind of payment. The mother had to agree to terminate her rights without having anything appear like they were buying her babies."

Cole pursed his lips and made a few notations in the notepad that he never seemed to be without. "Do you know the name of the administrator at Wings of Hope?"

Julie nodded. "Yes. His name is Greg Richmond. I got to know him when I was handling the adoption."

Cole scribbled the name down and then studied what he'd written before he looked up and smiled. "I guess that's all I wanted to ask you today. You've been very helpful, and we appreciate your time."

Julie rose to her feet, and Cole and Holly did so as

well. She walked back around her desk and extended her hand. "I'm glad to help in any way I can. Let me know if you have further questions, but I think I've told you all I know."

Holly shook Julie's hand and smiled. "Thank you for your help today and for all you did for Ruth and Michael."

"I only wish they were still with us so that they could see those babies grow up. But I know you're going to do a wonderful job with them, Holly."

"I'm going to try," she said. "It's difficult to balance all my commitments, but they're two welcome additions to my life."

"I'm sure they are," Julie said as she led them to the door.

She opened it, and they were about to step into the hall when Cole turned back to her. "One more question, Julie. Do you know a man named Willie Trask?"

Julie's brow wrinkled in thought, and then she slowly shook her head. "I don't think I've ever met anyone with that name. Is he connected to the twins in some way?"

"It's just a name that's come up in the investigation. It's probably nothing," Cole answered. "Let me know if you come across anything in your records that you think might be of help to us."

"I'll do that," Julie said, "and you two have a good day."

She closed her office door, and Cole and Holly walked down the hall and past the receptionist to the exit. Once outside, Holly turned to Cole. "She seemed very helpful."

"Yeah, she did. I can't figure out, though, how

I've never heard of Wings of Hope maternity home. I thought I knew most of the businesses in this county."

"Maybe it hasn't been there very long," Holly said.

"That could be. I think I need to take a drive over there and talk to this Greg Richmond."

Holly frowned. "What do you think he can tell you that Julie hasn't already explained?"

"I don't know, but I always like to double-check anyone connected to people who've been involved in a violent crime. And maybe this maternity home has nothing to do with the attacks, but if it all connects to the twins, then I want to talk to the person who arranged for Ruth and Michael to meet the mother in the first place."

Holly stared at him as she remembered how dedicated he'd always been to doing the right thing and wanting to help others do that, too. It was one of his qualities she'd always admired the most. "Thank you, Cole," she said.

A startled look flashed across his face, and he stopped and turned to face her. "For what?"

"For being the man you are. For being dedicated to seeing that justice prevails, for being the best man I've ever known, and for being here for me now just like you were years ago."

His Adam's apple bobbed, and he bit down on his lip. "Thank you for saying that." He paused a moment before he continued. "I know your visit to Jackson Springs has been troubling so far, but I have to tell you I'm glad you're here. I feel like we are mending some fences that we needed to fix years ago. I'm sorry we didn't."

She blinked back tears. "So am I."

They stared at each other before he reached for her hand and clasped it in his. Then they walked to the car, not talking but just enjoying this moment in time that had touched and healed both their hearts.

Cole pulled the car to a stop in the parking lot of the Wings of Hope maternity home and glanced over at Holly. She had been quiet on the drive from Jackson Springs, and he'd been content to enjoy the time with her as he pondered the things they'd said to each other earlier.

When he'd agreed for her to come with him today, he'd wondered if they would spend time trying to outrun reporters. But they had been able to slip out the back way just as Holly had said. So far, they hadn't been discovered, and he was glad. She needed some time when she could feel like a regular person going about her life without the prying eyes of the public focused on her.

"I guess your disguise is working today," he said as he turned off the engine.

She frowned as she glanced at him. "What disguise?"

He laughed as he chucked her under the chin. "No makeup, tennis shoes instead of cowboy boots, hair in a ponytail that's sticking through the back opening of a ball cap and sunglasses. Without your rhinestones and all that stage makeup you usually have on, you look like a girl I once knew."

She stuck her tongue out at him and reached for the door handle. "I take back all the nice things I said about you earlier."

"Too late," he called after her as she climbed out of the car. "I heard them, and I'm not letting them go."

They were both still smiling when they walked in the door of the maternity home. Right away, Holly was struck by the thought that the building seemed just like what its name implied—a home. They walked into a cozy reception area that could have passed for a living room in someone's house.

Comfortable furniture filled the room, and a colorful Persian rug covered the center of the hardwood floor. A fireplace on one side of the room seemed to be the focal point of the area with chairs arranged close to it. Magazines that would appeal to women were placed on tables throughout the room, and the pictures on the wall, from a field full of daisies to an eagle in flight, all offered scenes that seemed to soothe the soul.

A young woman sat behind a desk at the side of the room, and she smiled as they came in. "Good afternoon. May I help you?"

Cole pulled out his badge again. "I'm Detective Cole Jackson, and I'd like to speak with Mr. Richmond if he is in."

The girl didn't seem taken aback by the sight of a police officer at her desk and nodded. "Mr. Richmond was in his office a few minutes ago, but he has a meeting off-site not long from now. He may have already left. I'll go check."

With that, the young woman got up and walked out of the room. Once they were alone, Cole turned to Holly. "This looks like a nice place."

"Yeah, it does. I imagine it gives expectant mothers who are scared about the future a warm feeling when they walk in here."

Before he could answer her, the young woman was back. "You had good timing. He was just about to leave, but he says he can see you."

They followed her out of the room and down a hallway. About halfway down, she stopped at an open door and motioned for them to go in. A tall man, perhaps in his forties, rose from behind a desk and smiled as they entered. Cole expected him to shake hands with them but instead he indicated two chairs in front of him, and they all sat down.

Once they were settled, Greg Richmond let his gaze drift over them. "Miss Dennis said that a detective was here to see me." His gaze moved to Holly. "And you don't have to tell me who you are. You look so much like your sister."

Holly's face flushed, and she wiped her hands on her jeans. "I didn't think I'd be recognizable today. You must have a keen eye."

He laughed and shook his head. "No, just a huge fan who's followed your career for years. I was thrilled when I met your sister. She talked about you so much that I felt I came to know you." His eyes darkened. "I was sorry to hear about the plane crash. My thoughts have been with you and the children ever since."

"Thank you, Mr. Richmond."

Cole cleared his throat and leaned forward. "Actually, we're here today to talk to you about the twins. We understand that they were the children of a young woman in your care."

Greg reached out and picked up a pen from his desk and began to roll it between his fingers. His eyebrows pulled down across his nose, and he frowned.

"Yes. She was here for about three months before the babies were born. She didn't know she was going to have twins when she first came, and she really worried about their future when she found out it was two babies. She was so happy to know that her children were placed in a good home."

Cole's eyebrows arched. "She stayed here for three months? That must have been expensive. Julie Swanson told us that neither the mother nor the father had any family. How did she afford that?"

Greg smiled. "Because we are a 501C3 nonprofit organization licensed by the state. We accept payment from our clients who can afford it, but we never turn anyone away if they can't pay—we have funds to cover that."

"Oh, and how do you raise your money?"

"Well, as I said, we have some clients who pay. Then we have a marketing and development department that works constantly to raise funds. We have a black-tie gala once a year for supporters of our facility, and we sponsor a golf tournament every summer. But on top of that, we have an extensive list of previous donors, and we are constantly sending them news about the latest developments around here."

"Sounds like you run a well-oiled machine," Cole said.

Greg nodded. "We do, but I have the feeling you didn't come here to ask about the workings of our business. What did you really come for?"

"We wanted to know more about the twins' mother. There have been some problems with the twins for the last few days, and we're checking out a few things."

Greg's eyes grew round, and he sat up straight in his chair. "Are they having health problems? I can assure you our doctors pronounced them free of any disabilities when they were born."

"No, it's nothing like that," Cole hastened to inform him. "They have survived two kidnappings, and I'm trying to find out who might have a reason to do that."

"Kidnappings?" Greg slumped back in his chair and stared from Cole to Holly. "That's horrible."

Cole nodded. "I know."

He was silent for a moment as his gaze raked over Holly. "Do you think it's someone who knows you're a wealthy woman and wants to try to extort money from you?"

Holly shrugged. "We honestly don't know. We're exploring every possibility. It might be related to me, but it might not."

Greg looked back at Cole. "Do you have any suspects yet?"

"We have a person of interest. His name's Willie Trask. Do you happen to know him?"

"Willie Trask, Willie Trask," Greg murmured over and over before he shook his head. "I've never heard the name before. Who is he?"

"We don't know yet, but we'll find him," Cole answered before he looked down at his notepad. "One other thing. I understand how your facility works on payment for the care of the mothers, but do the women who give birth receive any monetary compensation for giving up their babies?"

"You mean being paid to terminate their rights?" Greg's face turned red. "That amounts to baby selling, and in Tennessee that is a Class C felony for all parties involved. I can assure you, Detective Jackson, that nothing like that occurred in this situation. Adoptive parents can pay any medical expenses not covered by insurance and for any counseling needed by the mother. Also, the adoptive parents can pay living expenses for ninety days before the birth of the baby and forty-five days afterward and for the counsel of an attorney if the birth mother wants one. Any money paid for these services should go through an attorney's office and should never be made as a direct payment to the mother. Since the birth mother in this case was receiving free room and board and medical care from our facility for the months before the birth and the first few weeks afterward, there was no need for living expenses or insurance. Also, we have licensed counselors on staff who work with the mothers after the adoption is finalized. So there wouldn't have been any reason for Michael and Ruth to pay anything."

"Do you ever have anyone who agrees to adoption and then changes her mind after the papers are signed?"

"The birth mother has three days after signing the agreement to terminate the adoption, and we've had one or two think they wanted to. In the end, though, they proceeded with the adoption because they had no way of taking care of their child."

"Did Ethan and Emma's mother consider changing her mind?"

Greg shook his head. "No, she didn't. She was happy that Michael and Ruth were taking the babies."

Cole tilted his head to one side and stared at Greg. "I understand she died."

"Yes, she did. Childbirth is so much safer than it was even fifty years ago, but there are still exceptions. She had a blood clot hit her heart. She died before we could save her."

"Did the autopsy reveal that she died of a blood clot?"

"There was no need for an autopsy," Greg said. "One of the doctors who volunteer their services to our home signed the death certificate and listed the cause."

"What did you do with the body?"

"She's buried in the Shady Lawn Cemetery in Jackson Springs."

Cole started to close his notepad but paused. "One more thing, Mr. Richmond. What was the name of the mother?"

Greg didn't say anything for a moment, and then he shook his head. "I don't know if I can tell you that or not. Our records are private, and even though the mother's dead, I think you'd have to have a court order to open them."

Cole flipped the notepad closed. "That's fine. I can get one if I need to." He rose to his feet and held out his hand. "Thank you for your time, Mr. Richmond. If I need anything else, I'll be in touch."

"Please do that, Detective," he said as he came around his desk. His gaze went to Holly. "It was very nice meeting you. I bought your new album last week, and the songs on it are great."

"Thank you, Mr. Richmond. I'm going on tour

soon. I'll send you some free tickets to my concert in Asheville."

His face lit up. "That would be wonderful. I'll look forward to it."

They walked back to the reception area and were almost to the door leading outside when a voice called out to them. "Wait just a minute, please."

Cole glanced over his shoulder at the receptionist, who had risen from behind her desk and was walking toward them. Her gaze was riveted on Holly. When she got near them she stopped and licked her lips. "Miss Lee, I recognized you the minute you walked in, and I couldn't let this opportunity pass without telling you I'm a huge fan."

Holly tilted her head to one side, and the smile that had always made his pulse race lit her face. "Thank you, Miss…"

"Dennis," she said. "Kathy Dennis."

Holly stuck out her hand. "It's nice to meet you, Kathy, and I appreciate your telling me you are a fan."

"Oh, yes," she gushed. "All your songs are favorites on my playlist. I'm hoping I get to attend one of your concerts on your next tour."

"Maybe you can. I just told Mr. Richmond I would send him some tickets for the Asheville concert on my upcoming tour. I'll be glad to include two for you and your boyfriend."

The girl's cheeks grew red. "Oh, Miss Lee. I'd appreciate that, but one ticket will be fine. I don't have a boyfriend."

Holly nodded. "I'll still send two. You can bring a

friend. But as pretty as you are, you'll probably have a boyfriend before long."

Kathy shrugged. "I don't know about that, but it's nice of you to say so. And let me say also that I was sorry about what happened to you at the concert here in Jackson Springs last night. I was there, but I wasn't outside in the mob that rushed you. I'm glad you weren't hurt."

"Thank you, Kathy. I enjoyed the concert. In fact, I saw a lot of promising talent there."

"My local favorite group was performing. I try to catch all their appearances."

"And which one was that?" Holly asked.

"The Mavericks. Do you remember them?"

Holly's eyebrows arched and she glanced at Cole. "Jason's band? How well do you know him?"

"Oh, I—I don't know him," she stammered, and Cole had a difficult time suppressing the laugh that rumbled in his throat. "I just think he's a talented musician."

Holly's mouth quirked as if she was also holding in a chuckle. "Well, it was nice meeting you, Kathy, and I'll send those tickets here."

"Thank you, Miss Lee."

"You're welcome, and you have a great day."

Cole opened the door, and he and Holly walked out of the maternity home without speaking and got in the car. Holly fastened her seat belt before she turned to him. "What did you think?"

He grinned. "I think Jason has a groupie."

She reached over and punched his arm. "Not that. What did you think about the things Greg Richmond said?"

He swiveled in his seat to face her and shook his head. "I don't know. Richmond talked a good game, but something about what he said didn't ring true."

"What do you mean? I thought he was very forthcoming."

"Yeah, he was. But there were two things that bothered me. One, I thought it was strange that we didn't see a single pregnant woman the whole time we were there."

"Maybe they were resting. After all, it is afternoon."

"That's a possibility, but also I didn't understand about his refusal to tell us the mother's name. Following her death, I'd think her privacy would be a moot point. But I could be wrong. I'll have to ask the lawyer who handles the town's affairs about it."

Holly stared through the windshield for a moment before she turned back to face him. "Maybe there's another way to find out who she was."

"How?"

"Surely Michael and Ruth had adoption papers, and they would have listed her name. I haven't had time to go through all of Michael's files yet, but maybe I need to do that now. Do you think it would help if we could identify her?"

Cole raked his hand through his hair. "At this point, I'm clutching at straws, and I don't know what's important and what's not. Maybe the adoption papers hold a key to something we're overlooking."

"Then I'll get started on finding those papers after dinner tonight." She bit down on her lip before she spoke again. "Would you like to help me look? You can eat with us, and then we can start our search."

He knew she was giving him the opportunity to refuse her invitation, but he didn't want to. Many times over the past years, he'd wondered where she was and what she was doing. Right now, she was back with him, and he was going to take advantage of every minute he could be with her.

Besides, it would give him some time with the twins. He'd missed being with them since Ruth's and Michael's deaths. They would be gone before long, and so would Holly. He'd do well to remember she wouldn't be here much longer.

With a sigh, he cranked the engine and darted a glance at her. "I'd love to, as long as you're not cooking."

A playful pout pulled at her mouth. "Cole Jackson, has anyone ever told you that you know how to deflate a girl's ego?"

He grinned. "Yeah. It's my defense mechanism against girls who are a thorn in my flesh."

Her eyes softened, and she reached over and trailed her finger down his cheek. "It's so easy to fall back into our old ways with each other, isn't it? It's almost like we've never been apart."

His stomach clenched at her touch. She was right. It was all too easy to pretend they were still those kids they used to be—the ones who were so in love. But he knew that was all in the past. Their lives were too different for anything to happen between them now. He cleared his throat and gently pushed her hand back into her lap.

"Almost," he said, "but not quite."

Her eyes darkened at his words, and he knew he had hurt her. But there was nothing else he could do.

When they found out who was after the twins, she would leave and he'd still be here. He had to protect his heart from being ripped to shreds a second time.

Slowly, he drove away from the maternity home.

EIGHT

By the time they arrived at the road that led from the highway through the back of the property, the afternoon sun was beginning its descent into the west. They hadn't talked much on the way home, and Holly didn't know what kind of mood Cole was in. Maybe she shouldn't have touched his cheek, but the way he'd stared into her eyes had evoked feelings she hadn't experienced in years.

Since leaving Jackson Springs, she had met many men who claimed to be interested in a relationship, but most of them only wanted to take advantage of her fame and her connections in the music industry. A few had been different, and there had been one who she really believed loved her. But she never could return his feelings for her. She'd decided at the time that her hesitance was because she was married to her career, but now, being back where her roots were, she knew it was the memory of Cole that had guarded her heart against anyone else.

The reality of the situation, though, was that he might still have fond memories of the years together, but he didn't want to rekindle their past. It appeared to be enough of a struggle just to accept her friendship, and his rejection of her earlier seemed to have only solidified his determination to steer clear of anything that might bring them closer.

She glanced over at him when he pulled to a stop at the house's back door and turned the engine off. "It's still a little early for dinner. Mrs. Green should be cooking right now. We can get started searching for the adoption papers if you want to come in, or you can come back later for dinner."

He exhaled a deep breath. "I'll check in with the station, but I don't think there's any need for me to go back there tonight. I might as well stay and get started on our search."

"Then come on in," she said as she exited the car.

He followed her as she climbed the steps to the back porch and gave a start of surprise when the door was pushed open from the inside. One of the newer security guards stepped aside for her to enter. "Good evening, Miss Lee. We were beginning to get worried about you."

"No need for that, Cal. I was with an officer of the law. How have things been around here?"

"Even with all the media out front it's been quiet. Todd and Ray are off tonight. So you have Brad and me."

She smiled at the young man and glanced over her shoulder at Cole. "This is Detective Jackson. He's going to have dinner with us. What time are you and Brad eating?"

"Oh, don't worry about us. Mrs. Green will see to us. You have a good evening, ma'am."

"Thanks. I will."

Once inside the house, Holly turned to him and said, "I'll go tell Mrs. Green we're here and check on the children. I won't be gone long."

"I'll go with you. I want to see the children."

Together they climbed the stairs to the nursery. When they walked in, Mandy stood over the twins and stared down at them as they played with some blocks that were scattered about the floor.

When they saw Holly and Cole, they both jumped to their feet. Holly grabbed Emma while Cole picked up Ethan. "What are you doing?" Holly asked as she kissed Emma's cheek.

Mandy chuckled. "They wanted the blocks, so I'm letting them play a bit before I take them downstairs for their dinner."

Cole dropped down to the floor, picked up a block and held it up to Ethan. "Hey, big guy, want to build something with me?"

The baby laughed and squirmed out of Cole's grip as he reached for another block. Holly looked at Emma and smiled. "Shall we join the party?"

Then she dropped down beside Cole, and for the next ten minutes the four of them sat on the floor building a tower. As soon as they'd get a few blocks stacked up, one of the twins would knock it down. They all would laugh and begin the process again.

Finally, Holly called a halt to the fun. "It's time for you two to have dinner. Let's go see what Mrs. Green has for you."

Mandy followed them to the kitchen as Holly and Cole carried the twins. Once there they settled them in their high chairs and Holly reached for Emma's plate, but Mandy stopped her. "Let me feed them.

I'm sure you and Detective Jackson have things to discuss. I'll let you know when they're ready for bed."

Cole stepped over and ran his hand over Ethan's head then touched Emma's cheek. "See you two later."

Before Holly could say anything, he turned and walked out of the room. She stared after him as he walked toward the den. After a moment she followed and found Cole standing at the window and staring outside. She wondered if he was regretting coming home with her. He'd seemed to have a good time with the babies, but now he looked as if he was a million miles away.

She stood at the den's entrance and watched him for a moment before she moved across the room to stand beside him. When she touched his arm, he jumped like she'd startled him. "I'm sorry. I didn't mean to scare you. What's so interesting out there?"

He sighed and rubbed the back of his neck. "I guess I was lost in thought. Nothing important." He inhaled a deep breath. "Are you ready to start the search?"

She wanted to push him more to tell her what he was thinking but she could still read him well enough to know when he wasn't ready to share his thoughts. She needed to get started looking for the adoption document. Then maybe he'd relax some.

She pointed to the desk. "Michael has some files in the desk drawers. Why don't you start there and see what you can find? There's a safe in Ruth and Michael's bedroom, and I have the combination in my room. That was the first thing I meant to clean out when I got here, but I haven't gotten around to it. I'll go up and do that while you're busy here."

He nodded but didn't say anything as he sat down at the desk and pulled several files out of one of the drawers. He looked up, and his eyes narrowed as if surprised that she was still standing there. "Do you need something else?"

"No," she said as she backed away from the desk.

Trying her best to stem the tears she felt forming, she walked out of the room with her back straight. For a while this afternoon, it had almost been like it was when they were growing up. They had laughed and joked, and then suddenly it had all changed. Now Cole was like the sullen stranger who had greeted her the night of the break-in. Maybe there was too much in their past for them to ever regain the friendship they'd once had.

She stopped in the hallway outside the den and braced her hand on the wall. She stood there a minute with her head bowed and a prayer on her lips. *Please, God,* she prayed, *forgive me for putting my dreams ahead of Cole and hurting him so badly. Show me how to make it up to him so he can forgive me.*

A sweet peace filled her as she raised her head. She didn't know how, but she was certain God was going to help her receive Cole's forgiveness. She just had to be careful and let Him guide her actions.

At the moment, however, she needed to look for those papers, and she headed upstairs to find the combination to the safe.

After retrieving the code from her room, she went back to her sister's bedroom and sat down on the floor in front of the small safe. Carefully, she entered the numbers and pulled the safe's door open.

She'd expected to find a stack of papers and maybe some personal items. There were a few, but not many. A ring box sat on top of the documents, and she pulled it out and opened it. Her eyes filled with tears when she saw her mother's wedding ring nestled inside the black velvet-lined box.

After a minute, she closed the box, set it aside and pulled out a sheaf of documents. She gripped the papers tightly as she pushed up from the floor and walked over to sit on the bed. One by one, she went through the pile, discarding out-of-date records that needed to be thrown away and laying documents of importance in a separate stack.

Just before she reached the bottom of the bundle, she picked up a legal-sized envelope that was packed with documents. Her eyes grew wide as she caught sight of the return address in the left-hand corner. It was Julie Swanson's office.

Carefully, she pulled out the papers and unfolded them. Her heart began to beat faster as she read through the court document that proclaimed Ruth and Michael had fulfilled all the legal requirements to adopt Emma and Ethan and the court had so ordered it. Included with the document were the babies' new birth certificates, changing their names to Emma and Ethan Whitson.

Holly let out an excited squeal and jumped up from the bed. Clutching the papers in her hand, she ran downstairs and into the den. Cole looked up when she burst into the room and rose from his chair. "What's the matter?"

She waved the papers over her head. "I found them! They were in the safe!"

He came around the desk and met her halfway into the room. "What do they say? What's the birth mother's name?"

Holly's mouth gaped open, and she stared down at the papers she held. "I was so excited I didn't look."

He reached for the documents and took them from her hand. "Then let's see if we can find it."

Together they sat on the couch, their heads almost touching, as they scanned the papers, looking for the name they needed. Suddenly, Cole stiffened. "Bingo! There it is!"

He pointed to a line, and Holly leaned forward to read the name scrawled there. "Teresa Wilson." She looked up at Cole. "That's all there is? No address? Just her name."

"Knowing her name is a start. Especially since we know where she's buried, because Greg Richmond told us. We can get the cemetery officials to find her grave on their map for us."

Holly frowned. "But why do we want to visit her grave? We didn't even know her."

"Because possibly her birth date is on the tombstone. If it is, then we can begin to do a search for more information about her. Maybe Willie Trask is someone from her past. You never know until you begin to dig." Cole riffled through the rest of the papers. "I see they put the new birth certificates in there, and whoa... What's this?"

Holly almost gasped at the sudden change of expression on Cole's face. He had suddenly turned pale, and his mouth hung slightly open as his eyes narrowed on a piece of paper in front of him. Holly inched closer to him. "Cole, what's the matter? What did you find?"

He held out the document, and she took it and then stared down at it. She couldn't believe what she was seeing. Her breath hitched in her throat, and for a moment, she thought she was going to be sick.

Her hand shook as she gave the piece of paper back to Cole. "I—I don't understand. How can this be?"

Cole shook his head. "I guess the question of whether or not any money changed hands in this adoption has just been answered." Holly wanted to argue, but there was nothing she could say. Not when she'd just handed over the receipt for a cashier's check signed by Michael and made out to Teresa Wilson in the amount of two hundred and fifty thousand dollars.

Cole couldn't believe what he held in his hand. To someone who lived on a policeman's salary, it seemed to him that his friend Michael had paid a small fortune to adopt two children. Besides being unable to comprehend why his friends would do such a thing, he couldn't understand where Ruth and Michael would have gotten that much money. They had been doing well with the ranch and the horses they bred and sold, but most of their wealth was tied up in the land and the ranching operations. It seemed hard to believe that they'd had that much money available on hand. And then it struck him. Somebody close to them would have been able to lay that much cash out without blinking an eye. Would she have willingly given him the money to make her sister happy?

He glared at Holly and shook the paper at her. "Was it you?"

Surprise flashed across her face, and she shrank away from him. "What are you talking about?"

"Did you give Michael the money to pay off Teresa Wilson, so they could adopt Emma and Ethan?" he thundered.

She jumped to her feet and clenched her fists at her sides. "Are you crazy? Of course I didn't give him the money."

He jumped up, too, and they stood almost nose to nose as they glared at each other. "Don't you realize that by giving that mother money, Michael broke the law? If you provided the money, you could be held liable, too."

"How dare you accuse me of such a thing. I didn't know anything about the money. Besides, I don't handle my money. My manager does. If he had given it to Michael, he would have told me so."

"Then where did he get it?"

She took a step closer to him and glared. "I don't know! Michael had an inheritance from his grandmother. Maybe that's where the money came from. I just know one thing. It. Did. Not. Come. From. Me!"

Cole turned away from her and raked his hand through his hair. "Holly, I don't know…"

He felt her hand on his arm, and he turned back to face her. Her eyes pleaded with him to believe her, and he wanted to. "I've never lied to you, Cole. Even when I left, I told you I was going, what I planned to do—and that I wouldn't be coming back. I want you to believe me now. I know nothing about this money."

He stared at her and then reached out and wrapped her in his arms. She came to him and pressed her face into his chest as her hands clutched his shirt. Her body shook, and immediately he felt ashamed of his harsh words toward her. He tightened his arms around her and kissed the top of her head.

"I know you wouldn't lie, Holly. I'm sorry. I'm just frustrated, because everywhere I turn I find more questions than I do answers. Please forgive me. I don't want to hurt you."

She tilted her head up and looked at him with tear-filled eyes. "I don't want to hurt you anymore, either. I'm so sorry I did. Can you ever forgive me for being selfish and wanting to follow my own dreams?"

He shook his head. "You weren't selfish any more than I was. I wouldn't give up my dreams to follow you, and you wouldn't give up yours to stay here with me. You had the wisdom to know that it wouldn't have worked out between us back then. If you'd stayed, you would have come to resent me, and if I'd gone, I would have come to resent you. I don't think our love would have been able to weather that. I guess it all worked out for the best in the long run."

Her gaze swept across his face, and his pulse quickened at the way her eyes seemed to be memorizing his features. "I miss you, Cole. I miss you so much."

"I miss you, too, darling. More than I can ever tell you." His voice came out husky, and he stopped himself before he said more that he might regret later. For now, though, he was holding Holly in his arms, and this time might never come again. Without second-guessing himself, he lowered his head and pressed his lips to hers. At first, she stiffened in surprise. Then her arms came up to circle his neck, and she returned his kiss with a hunger that matched his.

He didn't know how long they would have remained that way if it hadn't been for his cell phone ringing. He pulled back from Holly and glanced down at the caller ID, but she held him tighter. "Let it ring."

He shook his head. "I can't. It's the station."

She dropped her arms from around his neck, and he stepped back from her. "This is Cole. What is it, Brenda?"

He listened to what she was telling him, but he didn't want to believe it. When she finished, he said, "Tell Dan I'll meet him there. I'm leaving right now."

He disconnected the call and stared at the phone before slipping it back into his pocket. "I have to go," he said.

"Why? What did they want?" Holly asked.

He took a deep breath and shook his head. "Another unexpected problem has come up in this investigation."

Her eyes grew big. "What happened?"

"Sarah Palmer was shot and killed a few minutes ago."

Holly's hand grabbed at her throat, and she gasped. "How did it happen?"

"Brenda said Sarah stepped out on the back porch of the safe house, and someone shot her. They must have seen us take her there last night and were just waiting for their opportunity. I guess she was telling the truth after all. Somebody really was trying to kill her, and now they have."

NINE

By the next afternoon, Holly was about to go out of her mind. She hadn't heard from Cole, and she wanted to know more about Sarah Palmer's death. She'd almost called him several times but then thought better of it. He was involved in a murder investigation, and she didn't need to bother him. He would call her or come by when he had a chance. At least, she hoped he would.

All morning long, she and Mandy had kept busy as they carried on with Emma and Ethan's regular schedule. Breakfast, baths, diaper changes, snack, playtime, lunch and now nap time. She'd just settled on the sofa in the den when she heard footsteps and looked up to see Cole striding into the room.

She jumped to her feet and tried to downplay how happy she was to see him. "Hey, how are you? I've been worried, because I hadn't heard from you."

"I'm sorry," he said as he walked toward her. "It's been a crazy morning. The whole department is upset that someone was able to murder a potential witness we were trying to keep safe. The chief has made this case a priority. With her story about Emma and Ethan being in danger, it's put everybody on high alert."

She sat back down on the sofa, and he sank down beside her. "So, do you have any leads yet?"

He rubbed his hands over his red-streaked eyes and sighed. "I'm afraid not. Nobody saw anything. The staff at the safe house heard the shot and ran outside. She was lying on the back porch. They'd cautioned her earlier about staying inside, but she didn't listen. They're pretty shook up about it."

"I can understand," she murmured. "How about you? You look so tired."

"I'm fine. I got a few hours' sleep. I just grabbed a late lunch and thought I'd stop by and see how you're doing before I headed back to the station. I know this has been upsetting to you, too." He hesitated before continuing. "Sarah's murder is one more setback in this investigation. I can't seem to catch a break, and it's driving me crazy. This case is so important to me, because it involves you, and Ruth and Michael's children, and I want to solve it. But I don't know which way to turn right now."

She let her gaze drift over him, and her heart pricked at the tired lines she saw on his face. She reached over and wrapped her fingers around his arm. "Sometimes it helps to push your problems to the back of your mind and relax. Since you didn't get to have dinner with us last night, why don't you come back tonight?"

He stared at her for a moment, and she thought he was going to refuse. "Are you sure you want me to do that?"

"Of course I do. I wouldn't have asked if I hadn't meant it." A sudden thought popped into her head.

"On second thought, why don't we make it a party of sorts? You can bring Jason, and we can celebrate the success of his band's performance at the concert."

Cole studied her for a moment before he arched an eyebrow. "I've seen that look on your face before when you're up to something. Care to tell me what's really going on here?"

She grinned. "I guess you know me too well. It just seems to me that Jason is a nice guy, and I happen to know a young woman who would really like to meet him. Maybe we could arrange for that to happen tonight."

Cole closed his eyes and shook his head. "If I say no, you'll find some other way to get them together. So I'll see if Jason is free."

"Good," she said. "Call him now."

Cole mumbled something under his breath as he pulled his cell phone from his pocket and punched in a number. He frowned at her as he held the phone to his ear. "Jason," he said, "this is Cole Jackson."

He listened for a moment before he spoke again. "No, I don't need you for anything job-related. This is more of a social call. I'm over at Holly's house, and she was really impressed with your performance the other night. She'd like to tell you in person, though, and has asked you to come to dinner with me at her house tonight. Are you free?"

Holly couldn't tell from the expression on Cole's face what Jason was saying, but after a moment, he smiled. "Good. I'll pick you up about six o'clock. See you then."

He disconnected the call and frowned at Holly.

"Satisfied? You know I'm not much of a match-maker."

She laughed. "Oh, don't be such a fuddy-duddy. Now for Kathy. Do you have the number for Wings of Hope in your phone?"

"Yeah."

"Then give it to me, and I'll make the call to Kathy."

He handed it over, and a few minutes later, Holly smiled and ended the call. "She was excited to be invited to dinner at my house."

"You didn't tell her Jason was going to be here."

"No, and you didn't tell him, either. We'll introduce them when they arrive."

Cole shook his head and pushed to his feet. "Whatever. I'll see you later."

Holly smiled as he headed toward the door. "Looking forward to it," she called after him.

He didn't turn around but threw up his hand in dismissal as he'd always done when he was frustrated with her. It didn't matter, though. If Jason and Kathy hit it off, Cole might be glad they'd arranged this meeting. If they didn't like each other, then at least she'd tried.

She smiled as she headed to the kitchen to tell Mrs. Green they were going to have three guests for dinner.

At six thirty, Cole pulled the car to a stop in front of Holly's house and glanced over at Jason, who sat in the passenger seat. He felt like a traitor to the young man, who had no idea he was about to come face-to-face with a determined cupid. Cole sighed and shook his head. Truthfully, he could have refused to be a part of Holly's scheme, but he had to admit he was interested in seeing how the evening turned out.

"Well, here we are," he said as he opened his door and climbed out.

Jason did the same, and together they walked up the steps to the porch. Todd stood by the front door and studied them as they stepped up to the doorway. "Good evening, Detective Jackson. Miss Lee said to tell you to come on in when you got here. She's in the den."

"Thanks, Todd," he said as he opened the door and stepped into the entry.

Jason glanced at him and shook his head as they walked toward the den. "I can't believe I'm having dinner with Holly Lee."

Cole gave a snort of disgust. "She's just a normal woman like you see every day. She wouldn't want you to think differently."

Jason laughed. "She may seem like a normal woman to you, because you've known her a long time, but to me, she represents how a girl from a small town can make it big in the music industry. It gives guys like me hope that it can happen for us."

"It didn't just happen for her, Jason. She worked hard for it, and she gave up a lot to get where she is today."

Jason didn't reply as they stepped into the den. Holly looked up from the desk where she'd been staring at the computer screen and smiled as they came in. "Cole, Jason. I'm so glad you're here. I was just checking emails. I had an interesting one from Keith Jefferson that I think you might be interested in,

Jason." Cole took a second to make the connection, but then he remembered—Keith Jefferson was the lead singer of that band Jason was a fan of, Attitude.

Jason's eyebrows shot up, and he stared at Holly. "Why would I be interested?"

"Because the audio guys at the convention center sent me a video of your performance the other night, and I forwarded it to Keith. He really liked it and he wants to meet you and your band members."

Cole thought for a moment from the look on Jason's face that he might pass out. "H-he wants to meet us?"

Holly laughed and nodded. "He asked me to send him your contact information so he can set up a time for your band to come to Nashville and audition for him."

Jason's face grew even paler. "Audition?"

"Yeah. He's looking for some new acts to open for his band on their next concert tour. Are you interested in going to play for him?"

"Are you kidding?" His loud answer seemed to bounce off the walls. He grabbed Holly's hands and squeezed. "I can't believe this. Thank you, Miss Lee. Thank you, thank you, thank you."

She laughed. "You can thank me by being prepared when you go and making a good impression on Keith. After all, I pride myself on spotting emerging talent, and I don't want you to prove me wrong."

"You don't have to worry. We'll be ready." He glanced over at Cole. "I still can't believe it. We have a chance to play for Keith Jefferson."

Before Cole could reply, a sound from the door caught their attention. They looked around to see

Todd standing there with Kathy Dennis by his side. "Miss Lee, your other guest is here."

Kathy looked to be frozen in place. She stood there, her mouth gaping open, and stared at Jason as if she couldn't believe her eyes. Cole glanced at Jason and almost laughed out loud at the way he was looking at Kathy. Before anyone could say anything, Holly rushed over and grabbed Kathy's hand.

"Come in, Kathy. I'm so glad you're here." She put her arm around the girl's waist and pulled her into the room. "I have a friend I'd like to introduce you to. Of course, you already know Detective Jackson, and this is Jason Freeman." She turned to Jason. "Jason, this is Kathy Dennis. She's a big fan of your band and goes to see you perform all the time."

A smile broke across Jason's face as his gaze raked over the girl. "Is that right? It's great to meet someone who likes our music."

"Oh, I do," she gushed. "I thought your performance at the convention center was out of this world."

"You were there?"

Kathy nodded. "I came just to hear your band play. I think I've been to every performance you've done locally in the last year."

Jason's grin widened as he stepped closer to Kathy. "Sounds like you're the type of fan we hope to attract. Do you live in Jackson Springs?"

"Yes. I've been here about two years now."

Holly cleared her throat and grasped Cole's arm. "If you'll excuse me, I'm going to see how Mrs. Green is coming along with the dinner. You two stay here and get acquainted, and Cole can help me in the kitchen."

Her thinly veiled attempt to get the two young people alone wasn't lost on him, and he nodded. "Lead the way, Holly. I can hardly wait to see what you need help with."

He followed her to the door, and they both looked over their shoulders at Jason and Kathy, who had settled on the sofa and were already absorbed in a deep conversation. "I have to hand it to you, Holly," he said. "A professional matchmaker couldn't have done a better job. Jason seems completely taken with Kathy already—which makes me feel better since I felt like I was leading a lamb to the slaughter."

Holly looked up at him and laughed. "Don't be silly. This may be the start of something big."

An hour later, Cole stared at Holly across the dinner table and smiled. He and Holly might as well have been in another room for all the attention the others paid to them during the meal. From all appearances, it seemed that Jason and Kathy had taken an instant liking to each other. They chatted all during dinner, and Holly and Cole had been interested observers who merely smiled at each other from time to time.

With the meal over, Holly pushed her chair back and stood. "Let's go back in the den and have coffee. I'll check with Mrs. Green and tell her we're ready. I'll join you in a minute."

Cole followed Jason and Kathy back to the den and took his seat in one of the chairs. Holly came in a little later and sat down opposite him. "I'm sorry to be so long. I was upstairs helping Mrs. Green and Mandy get Emma and Ethan ready for bed. We're going to have to wait on the coffee for a few minutes."

She'd no sooner finished speaking than Mandy appeared at the doorway holding Ethan, Mrs. Green right behind her with Emma. "I thought you might like to tell these little ones good-night before we tuck them in."

Holly rose and met Mandy as she entered the room to take Ethan from her. A big smile covered her face as she nuzzled the baby's head and kissed him. Ethan's giggles rang out, and he squirmed in Holly's arms. Still holding Ethan, Holly turned her attention to Emma and plastered kisses all over the blond curls on her head.

Both babies struggled to get down, but Holly shook her head. "No, no. It's bedtime. No more playing tonight."

Cole got up and was about to step over to the twins, but before he could, Kathy stood and walked over to face Holly. She leaned forward and wrapped her fingers around Ethan's small hand. "You are so precious," she cooed. Then she turned her attention to Emma. "And you look so much like your mother. You're going to be a beauty just like she was."

Kathy's words startled Cole, and he stared at her for a moment. "I forgot you knew their birth mother."

Kathy nodded. "Yes. She was with us for a few months before the babies were born. During that time, we became friends. She felt so alone, and she worried so much about what to do. One day she was going to give them up, and then the next day she was going to keep them. She went back and forth for weeks until she decided to let Holly's sister and brother-in-law adopt them."

Holly's eyes had grown wide, and she stared at Kathy. "But she decided to give them up."

"Yes, she did. And your sister and brother-in-law were so thrilled when Mr. Richmond let them know her decision. I was the one who called them when Teresa went into labor. They came and waited outside the delivery room until the twins were born. I still tear up when I remember how happy your sister looked when she held them for the first time. She sat down in a chair, and the nurses handed her the babies. She cradled them, one in each arm, and cried."

Cole could tell Holly was about to lose her composure at the description of her sister and the babies together for the first time. She cleared her throat and blinked. "She called me that day. She was very happy."

Kathy nodded. "She was. That's why I was so worried about her when Teresa changed her mind about giving them up."

There was a sudden chill that penetrated the room, and Holly's startled gaze met Cole's. "She decided to keep them?" he asked.

"Yeah. The second day after they were born, she came to me and told me that she'd decided she wasn't giving them up."

Cole glanced at Holly, and the shocked look on her face made his stomach clench. "What did Mr. Richmond have to say?"

"I don't know. I didn't talk to her after that, but I knew she had three days after signing the papers. Since she'd signed the day they were born, she was still within the time frame to stop the adoption." Her eyes darkened, and she bit down on her lip. "But it didn't make any difference since she died later that afternoon. The doctor said it was a blood clot." She patted the cheek of each baby. "I'm just glad you two have someone to take care of you now."

Cole noticed Holly's arms tighten around Ethan, pulling him closer. "Yes, they have me now."

For a moment, he didn't know if she was going to say anything else. Then she handed Ethan back to Mrs. Green. "I think it's time these two were in bed. Mrs. Green, you can help Mandy get them down, and I'll see about the coffee."

She and Mandy headed up the stairs to get the twins settled. When they disappeared upstairs, Holly took a deep breath and forced a smile on her face. "Now, if you'll all have a seat, I'll go make the coffee."

"I really need to take off," Jason said, stopping her before she could leave. "My band is practicing tonight, and I told them I'd be there. Thanks for dinner, Holly. It was delicious." He turned to Kathy. "I rode with Cole, so my car's not here. Would you mind driving me? If you'd like, you can hang out with us while we practice and tell me what you think."

Kathy's eyes sparkled. "I'd love to." She turned back to Holly. "Thank you for dinner, and thank you for everything else, too."

Her meaning wasn't lost on Cole, and he smiled even though his mind was still whirling from what Kathy had just told them. He watched as Holly walked them to the door to see them out, calling after them, "Have a good night, you two. And, Jason, don't forget to text me your contact information."

"I won't. Thanks again."

Cole waited in the den for Holly to return. When

she did, she walked over and collapsed on the sofa. "Do you think Kathy was telling the truth about Teresa?"

He nodded and sat down beside her. "I do. The words just flowed so freely, and I don't think she had any idea that she was giving us information that we didn't know."

"But you asked Greg Richmond if Teresa changed her mind, and he said no. Why would he lie about that?"

Cole shook his head. "He may not have known. Kathy said Teresa told her she was going to tell Richmond the adoption was off, and then the blood clot came out of nowhere. She may have died before she spoke to him. What seems strange to me is the timing—that the day she made her decision to stop the adoption she suddenly died of a blood clot. After that, there was no need to stop the adoption."

"Are you saying you have doubts about the way she died?"

Cole shrugged. "At this point, it would be pure speculation, but I do know there wasn't an autopsy done. The doctor put the cause of death on the death certificate. With this new information, I think it warrants looking into more carefully."

"What are you going to do?"

"First thing in the morning," he said, "I'm going to present my suspicions to a judge and get a court order to have Teresa Wilson's body exhumed for an autopsy. Then we'll know the exact cause of death and where we go from there."

TEN

When Cole hadn't called by noon the next day, Holly was beginning to get worried. Maybe he was still trying to get permission to exhume Teresa's body. She couldn't stop her mind from racing ahead. Even if they were able to do an autopsy and there were any suspicious findings, that still didn't answer the question of who might have been involved.

At this point, the only thing that Cole seemed to be convinced of was that everything revolved around Emma and Ethan. Holly tried to swallow the lump that seemed to have lodged in her throat, but it was no use. Her babies were in trouble, and she didn't know what to do about it.

Her babies? It was still a little surprising every time she had that thought. Emma and Ethan had been Ruth's children, and all she had expected to be was the aunt who dropped into their lives every once in a while and spoiled them rotten for a few days. Since she'd become their guardian, that had begun to change. They were the children she thought she would never have, and she loved them with a fierceness that couldn't be rivaled. That was why it was so important to find out why a cloud of danger had descended on two helpless babies.

With a sigh, she looked at her watch. It seemed the morning had dragged by. She needed something to occupy her mind for the afternoon until she heard from Cole. A sudden thought hit her, and she pursed her lips. The mystery of where Michael and Ruth had gotten the money they'd paid for the adoption had never been solved. There had to be something around that would answer that question.

A possibility occurred, and she smiled. The safe. Maybe there was something inside that she had overlooked when she'd found the adoption papers. She ran to the stairs and took them two at a time and then rushed to the bedroom.

The code still lay where she'd left it, and she grabbed it and punched in the numbers. When the door swung open, she looked inside. Just as she'd suspected, several envelopes still lay on the bottom. She picked them up and shuffled through them but paused at the last one and stared at the return address.

Her breath hitched in her throat as she opened the envelope's flap and read the letter inside. It was from the lawyer in Atlanta who had handled Michael's grandmother's estate. The document confirmed that he, as the executor of the trust fund Michael had inherited, had approved the transfer of two hundred fifty thousand dollars to Michael.

Holly sat there for a few minutes and stared at the letter. The question was finally answered, but it brought no satisfaction to her. Tears gathered in the corners of her eyes. She'd never realized how desperate her sister and brother-in-law must have been for a baby.

She didn't know how long she sat there, but suddenly the ringing of her cell phone jerked her from her thoughts. She sighed in relief that Cole's number showed up. She put the phone to her ear.

"Cole. I've been going out of my mind wondering what was happening."

A soft chuckle rippled in her ear. "And hello to you, too, Holly."

"I'm sorry. I've just been so anxious to hear from you. So, a belated hello to you, too." She took a breath. "Now tell me, were you successful getting the court order?"

"I was. The judge signed the order, and I'm on my way to the cemetery now. I've already called, and they have the location of the grave. The work crew is waiting out there for me, but I wanted to let you know what was going on."

"Thank you. What happens when they've recovered the body?"

"It'll be sent to the coroner for an autopsy. He'll compare his results to the death certificate that the doctor signed. Once we have that done, we'll know how to proceed."

Holly sighed and rubbed her hands over her eyes. "How long is all of that going to take?"

"I don't know, Holly. I can't rush these things. Investigations take time."

A sudden rush of anger filled her. She wanted the twins safe, and she wanted it now. "Well, I don't have a lot of time. Your department needs to hurry this along, so I can get Emma and Ethan settled in our life in Nashville."

He was quiet for a moment, and when he spoke his

words were stilted. "I'm sorry we haven't been able to please you, but our department doesn't have the funds like big-city law enforcement has. If you need to get back to Nashville, then you should go. Whether you stay or leave makes no difference to our investigation. It will go on until we have some answers."

This conversation had taken a turn she hadn't intended it to, and she bit down on her lip at the curt tone of his words. The last thing she wanted was to alienate Cole again. On the other hand, maybe he was right that she didn't need to stay. She wanted to help with the investigation, but she had two children to think of, and it would be easier to keep them safe in Nashville. Her home there was less isolated and better secured. Maybe they needed to leave Jackson Springs.

"I know you're a good investigator, and in time, I have no doubt you'll find the answers you're looking for. As for me and the twins, it might be better if we went back to Nashville. My security team can keep us safe. Instead of worrying about our safety, you can concentrate on the case."

He was silent for a moment. "I haven't minded helping keep you safe. Even with all the trouble you've had here, I've enjoyed being with you again. I guess I just forgot for a moment that it was temporary. I'm sure you have more pressing obligations than hanging around the town you couldn't wait to leave."

The anger she'd felt a moment ago vanished at the hurt she heard in his voice. Why had she lashed out at him? All he'd done since she'd been home was try to help her, and she'd found herself coming to depend on him again.

Her eyebrows arched, and she suddenly knew why she'd spoken the way she had. She was scared. Scared that her old feelings for Cole were beginning to return, and she didn't know what to do about that. She had a life and a career, one that she'd worked hard to carve out for herself. Becoming close to Cole again threatened to destroy that. She couldn't let that happen.

She took a deep breath in an effort to calm her shaking body. "I'm sorry I spoke sharply to you, Cole. I appreciate everything you've done for us since we've been here, but I think it's time the twins and I went home."

He was silent for a moment, and she tightened her grip on the phone. "When are you going to leave?"

"I don't know. Probably in a few days."

"What about the house? I thought you were going to try to sell it."

"I am, but my manager can take care of that for me."

"It sounds like you have it all figured out. But then, you always did. If I don't see you before you leave, you take care of yourself. It was good seeing you again."

She knew he was getting ready to disconnect the call, and she couldn't let him go yet. "Cole, wait!"

"What is it, Holly?"

"I wanted you to know I found out where Michael and Ruth got the money they paid for the twins."

For the next few minutes she told him about finding the letter. When she finished, he sighed. "So that's where it came from."

"Yes," she said. "I wanted you to know so that you wouldn't think I'd given it to them."

When he spoke, his voice sounded sad. "I believed you when you told me you didn't give it to them. I know you wouldn't lie. Take care of yourself, Holly."

"Cole," she said, but it was no use. He'd already disconnected the call.

She sat there for a moment and stared at the phone, and her heart felt like it was about to break at the hurt she'd heard in Cole's voice. No matter what had happened in the past, he would always be an important part of her life.

Even with all the trouble she'd had since coming back to Jackson Springs, she'd been more content than she'd been in a long time. Being with Cole had brought joy into her life, and she knew she'd never fully fallen out of love with him. There would never be another man for her, and she was going to miss him when she was gone. But what could she do? Was there any way they could settle their differences and make a life together? And would Cole even want to?

Her heart screamed at her to call him back, but her head told her it was no use. She'd burned that bridge when she left ten years ago, and it was better to let it remain the way it was—her in Nashville and him in Jackson Springs.

She was about to slip the phone back in her pocket when it rang again. Hope flared that it might be Cole calling her back, but it wasn't. The number for her manager, Aiden Hudson, showed up on the caller ID. She placed the phone to her ear.

"Hi, Aiden. I'm surprised to hear from you today. I thought you were taking a few days off."

"As if I have time to take off," he huffed.

Holly couldn't help but smile. She could imagine what he looked like—a scowl on his face and his hair standing on end from where he'd been running his hands through it. Although Aiden was an impeccable dresser, by this time of day his tie usually hung around his neck unknotted, his jacket thrown haphazardly across a chair while he talked on the phone, pacing back and forth across the room. It seemed like the man always moved like a whirlwind as he managed the needs of his clients. But it was no secret that she was his most lucrative one, and he had guided her career to where it was. She owed him a lot for taking a young starry-eyed musician and turning her into an award-winning artist.

"I'm glad you called," she said. "I wanted to update you on what's been going on here."

For the next few minutes, he listened as she related the latest developments in the case. "I should be there," he said when she was finished. "Or better yet, you should come back here. I didn't want you to go back to that town, and I was right. Now it's time for you to get back where you belong."

Even though she didn't want to agree, she knew she had to. "You're right. It's time I came home."

"When do you think you'll be ready to leave?"

"I don't know. Maybe a few days."

"Good," he said. "That fits in with what I was going to talk to you about."

His voice had taken on the tone that it always did when he was about to try to convince her of something he thought she wouldn't like. She sighed in exasperation. "Okay, Aiden. What is it this time?"

"Something I think you'll enjoy doing. I had a call from the producer of that morning show on TV called *Live with the Davenports*."

"The one with the twin sisters who do stories about celebrities?"

"That's the one. This producer thought it might be fun for the sisters to interview a celebrity who has twins. Since you just acquired a set after their parents were killed, they want to do an interview."

Holly closed her eyes and shook her head. She didn't like doing TV appearances, but she realized they were important as someone who depended on fans' opinions. A refusal to do interviews had sunk many careers in the past, and she'd always endeavored to ensure that it didn't happen to her.

"Okay," she said. "Tell them I'll be back in Nashville by the end of the week, and I'll be glad to do the interview."

Aiden cleared his throat. "Well, that's just it, Holly. They don't really want to do a traditional interview. They want to play up 'the twins' angle, and how you're making out with your new responsibilities. They want to see you interacting with the babies, and how they're making out after losing their parents."

Holly sat up straighter and shook her head. "No way. You know how I feel about keeping them out of the spotlight. The Davenports can interview me, but they can't use Emma and Ethan."

"Take a minute to think about this," he wheedled. "We're talking about the number one morning show on network TV. You're getting ready to perform on a cross-country tour. I've signed contracts at the different venues, and we need those stadiums packed if we are going to keep from ending up in the red. I can't do the publicity for you. I can only line it up. You're the one who has to show up and do the work."

Holly gritted her teeth and shook her head, frowning. How many times had he said those same words to her, and they worked every time. She was the one who had wanted this life. She was the one who had given up the only man she would ever love. Now she was stuck with her choice.

She exhaled a deep breath, and her body sagged in defeat. "Okay, Aiden. Do they want to do the interview at my house in Nashville?"

"Actually," he said, "they want to do it in Jackson Springs."

Her eyebrows shot up. "Jackson Springs? Why?"

"They're going to show your roots. You know, the town where you lived, your childhood home, the story about your sister's death and you becoming the guardian of twins. They want to show how a celebrity manages a career while becoming a mother overnight to two children. They want to follow you around for a day and see you interacting with them. I've arranged for them to be there day after tomorrow."

"You scheduled this without asking me first?" Her surprised words echoed in the room.

"Of course I did. As I said, it's my job to set up the publicity and…"

"Yeah, I know," she said, "and mine to show up. So what time should I expect them?"

"They'll be there around eight o'clock. They want to see your morning routine with the twins. Then they want to go to that park downtown, the one where you used to do summer concerts when you were in school. They thought it would be a nice touch to show you having an outing with the babies in a place that holds such fond memories for you."

An uneasy feeling swept over her. "I don't know about that, Aiden. With all that's been going on, I don't know if it's safe to take Emma and Ethan out in public."

"Don't worry about it. We've arranged to close the park off to visitors for about an hour, and I've made sure your security team will be in place. You'll have nothing to worry about."

She still didn't like the idea of exposing the children to possible harm again—the supermarket incident was still fresh in her mind—but it should be okay if the security team did their job. Besides, who would take the risk of attacking when a full camera crew would catch their every move? After a moment, she exhaled a deep breath. "Okay, I'll be expecting them day after tomorrow."

"Good," he said before he disconnected the call.

Holly stared at the phone a few minutes, replaying the conversation in her mind. Aiden had always been able to talk her into what he wanted, but she had to admit he'd never steered her wrong. If he thought this TV interview would promote her tour, she would have to go along with it. But she couldn't shake the feeling that taking the twins to the park wasn't a good idea.

Maybe she should call Cole and ask him what he thought. Then she thought better of it. He didn't want to be bothered; his hanging up on her had told her as much. He was out of her life, and there was no going back. Now all she had to do was find a way of living with that decision.

Cole had been unable to sit still all afternoon after talking with Holly. He'd stormed out of the office as soon as he'd hung up and headed to the cemetery. It didn't take but a few minutes to find the crew who'd come to dig up the grave. The machinery was already humming as the shovel on the end of the crane dislodged large chunks of dirt and grass.

He paced back and forth a few feet back from where the men were working as he watched the scene unfold. A loud thud sounded as the scoop collided with something.

"We have it!" one of the men shouted, and the crew moved in to finish their task.

Cole watched as they carefully removed the casket and checked the name for accuracy. Everyone was silent as the crew carried the remains of Teresa Wilson to the waiting hearse.

They slid the casket into the back of the vehicle and slammed the door, but none of them moved. Cole wondered how many times these men had been called on to perform this task. He expected them to turn and walk away but was surprised when the man who had appeared to be in charge throughout the operation took off his hat and held it over his chest. The other men did the same, and they stood there staring at the closed door.

Then the foreman began to speak. "Dear God, Your word says, 'In the sweat of thy face shalt thou eat bread, till thou return unto the ground; for out of it wast thou taken: for dust thou art, and unto dust shalt thou return.' We ask Your blessing on all those who will now receive the body of Your child, that they will treat her with respect and return her safely to the place of her eternal rest. Amen."

The amens of all the workers drifted across the quiet cemetery, and Cole felt his throat close with emotion. He added his own prayer that the doctors who now had charge of Teresa Wilson would find any hidden secrets about her death.

The health-department official, who'd been on-site to make sure the exhumation was carried out properly, stepped over to Cole as the hearse pulled away. "I'll tell the medical examiner that we need a report on this as soon as possible. But even so, it should take a day or two to get the results."

Cole nodded. "That's what I figured. Tell him to send a copy of the report to me when he has it completed."

"Will do," the man said before he turned and headed toward his car.

Cole didn't move but stared at the vacant grave for a few minutes as he pondered the developments in the case that had started with Holly discovering an intruder in the twins' nursery. He would never have suspected that what happened that night would lead to him standing at an empty grave and wondering what secrets it had held. Maybe he would have answers to that question in a few days.

Without thinking, he pulled his phone from his pocket and was about to call Holly and give her an update when he remembered he didn't need to do that. She'd made it clear to him that she was leaving and no longer intended to keep up with the investigation.

By the time he received the autopsy report, Holly would be back in Nashville, and he would be alone in Jackson Springs the way he had been for the past ten years. Once again, he stared up at the sky as he had done so many times in the past and silently asked God why He'd allowed him to fall in love with a woman he never would be able to keep.

But just as it had happened in the past, there was no answer to his question.

ELEVEN

Holly had gotten up early so she could be sure to have everything ready for the Davenport sisters when they arrived. If she was honest with herself, though, she'd admit that she really hadn't slept much last night or the night before. It had been two days since her conversation with Cole, and she missed him more than she would ever have thought. Several times, she'd picked up her phone to call him but then had thought better of it. Things were settled between them, and she shouldn't do anything to change that.

She stopped scurrying around, placed her hands on her hips and surveyed the nursery. Everything was in place, and it was time to get this interview over with. This thought had just popped into her head when Mandy and Mrs. Green walked in, each holding a baby.

Holly rushed over and gave each of them a kiss. "How're my sweeties this morning?" she purred as she patted each of the curly heads.

They both let out a garbled stream of gibberish that sent a thrill through her. It wouldn't be long before they would be walking, then they'd be talking, and before she knew it, they would be going to their first prom. She promised herself that she wasn't going to miss one moment of their growing up and ignored the voice that whispered the question in her head, *How are you going to be there for every milestone if you continue touring ten months out of the year?*

Emma squirmed in Mandy's arms and reached out toward Holly. "Come here, darling," she said.

She'd just taken the baby when Todd appeared at the door. "The TV crew is here to begin setting up, Miss Lee."

After that, it was a madhouse of activity for the rest of the morning. The twins handled the hustle and bustle well, but Holly was still very thankful when the director finally called for a lunch break.

Sonya Davenport smiled as she rose from the chair where she'd been sitting. "I know this has been difficult, Holly, but it's almost over. All we have left is the visit to the park."

Holly nodded. "Emma and Ethan take a nap after lunch."

"That sounds good," Sonya said. "After they wake up, give us a call with a time frame, and we'll meet you at the park. We'll get a few shots of the three of you playing together, maybe you pushing them on the baby swings, and then call it a wrap."

Mandy and Mrs. Green had already taken the twins to the kitchen, and Holly waited until the film crew gathered all their equipment to leave. Then she led the two young men who'd been filming all morning downstairs. At the front door, they stopped and turned to her.

The one who seemed to be the main cameraman

smiled at her before exiting. "I don't think Miss Davenport introduced us when we got here. My name is Stephen Blakemore." He nodded toward the other young man. "And this is my assistant, Mark Hatfield. I really enjoyed filming you. Some people have the features that make the camera love them, and you're one of them. I look forward to seeing you this afternoon at the park."

Holly smiled. "Thank you, Stephen. I'm excited about filming our outing. See you then."

She closed the door behind him and stood in the entryway for a few minutes. Muffled voices came from the kitchen, and every once in a while, she could hear Ethan squeal in laughter at something Mandy had said.

As she stood there, she realized that she had everything she once thought she wanted. She had an amazing career, a fabulous mansion in Nashville and two children whom she loved with all her heart. The problem was, however, that she didn't have everything she needed. And that was someone to love her and share her life with. As she stood there, the thought of continuing to live on the road, going to one performance after another for the rest of her life, filled her with dread. She wanted a man she could love and one who would love her. A man that she could come home to at the end of the day.

It was then she realized she had made a mistake. Instead of reaching for what would truly make her happy, she had thrown it away just as she had done ten years ago. This time, there was no getting it back.

Tears streamed down her face, and she stumbled back into the den and sank down in a chair. As she sat there, her gaze drifted to the table beside the sofa, and she spotted her mother's Bible that lay on it. Ruth had treasured that Bible and had read it every day. She, on the other hand, hadn't even looked at one in years.

She'd once been close to God, but she had gradually lost track of that when she left home for Nashville. As if she had become focused only on herself. Once, she'd been filled with a joy that had come from loving God, but through the years that had slowly disappeared until she was consumed by loneliness.

She reached over and picked up the Bible and began to thumb through it. Suddenly, she stopped at a page where a verse was highlighted in yellow as her mother often did. A notation in ink beside the verse was dated during the summer when Holly was ten years old. She remembered that time well because it was the summer their mother had taken her and Ruth to their grandparents' home. They'd been there for several months while her parents tried to decide whether they wanted to divorce or not. Finally, they had decided to try again, and their family had been reunited.

Holly had often wondered what might have been the deciding factor in bringing her parents back together. As she read the verse her mother had marked, she thought she had found the answer. The words were from the book of Ezekiel and read, *A new heart also will I give you, and a new spirit will I put within you: and I will take away the stony heart out of your flesh, and I will give you an heart of flesh.*

As she thought about those words, she remembered how her parents' attitudes toward each other and toward her and Ruth had changed after they had come back home. The love that had once lived in their home had returned and flourished in her parents' marriage until death parted them.

If God had changed their hearts, then He could change hers also. She didn't want to have a stony heart anymore. She wanted to open up to love, and she wanted Cole to know that she loved him and always would. Whether or not he would return that love, she didn't know, but she knew she had been the one to shatter it. If it was to be mended, it was up to her to do it.

Her heart hammered in her chest as she pulled her cell phone from her pocket and punched in his number. To her surprise, it went straight to voice mail: "You have reached the number of Cole Jackson. This is the day the Lord has made, and I hope you're having a blessed one. I'm away from my phone right now, but if you'll leave a message, I'll get back to you as soon as I can."

Disappointed, she waited for the beep. "Cole, this is Holly. I know I treated you terribly the last time we spoke, but I've finally come to grips with what my heart has always told me. I love you, and I don't want to leave. All it will take to make me stay is one word from you. I hope to hear from you."

She ended the call and slipped the phone back in her pocket. Now it was up to him. Maybe he would call. But first, she had to get through the afternoon at the park. For some reason, she wished he knew about the plans to take the twins out in public.

She still didn't feel comfortable with the idea, but

it was too late to back out now. All she wanted was to get through it safely and return home.

It had been two days since Cole had spoken with Holly. In some ways, her decision to leave Jackson Springs had upset him more this time than it had when she'd left ten years ago. Back then, he had held on to the hope that she might return, but this time he knew she wouldn't. She had a wildly successful life in Nashville now, and she was never going to be a part of his world again. He didn't know how he was going to do it, but he had to put her out of his mind once and for all.

Maybe he could at least forget about her for a few hours, so he could catch up on work. It had probably piled on his desk while he was in court this morning. Court appearances were a necessary part of his job, and he'd been happy to present the evidence in a robbery case that he and Dan had closed a few weeks ago. But he always dreaded what awaited him when he returned to the office.

Today is going to be no different, he thought as he strode through the front doors at the sheriff's department. An afternoon of listening to messages, returning phone calls and following up on recent arrests was what he had to look forward to, and the sooner he got to it the better off he would be. Then maybe he could go home, relax… He might even be able to get a good night's sleep tonight—he hadn't had one since he last spoke with Holly.

As he entered the department's reception area, he remembered that he hadn't turned his phone on since leaving the courthouse. He pulled the phone from his pocket, powered it up and frowned at the display of missed calls. He scrolled through them but paused when he saw Holly's number. Not only had she called but she'd left a message.

His finger hovered over the button for a moment as he decided whether or not he wanted to listen to what she had to say right away. He was about to connect to the voice mail when Brenda looked up from behind her desk and spotted him.

"Cole," she called out. "I didn't realize you were back."

"Just got here. Court went a little longer than I thought it would. Anything interesting going on around here?"

She nodded and pushed her glasses up on her nose. "Yeah. You got a call from Dr. Hunt, the medical examiner. He said he's finished the autopsy, and he needs to see you right away."

Cole's eyebrows arched. "He wants me to come to his office?"

"That's what he said."

Cole glanced down at the phone again and debated listening to Holly's voice mail before he left. What if she'd had some kind of emergency? She could have been attacked again.

No, he told himself. That was hardly likely. If there was an emergency, she'd have called nine-one-one rather than leaving a message for him. Whatever she was calling about, it probably wasn't urgent. He decided that he needed to check out the autopsy results first and shoved his phone back in his pocket.

"I'll be at his office if anyone needs me," he said as he turned and headed back out the door.

Ten minutes later, one of Dr. Hunt's assistants ushered him into the room where the autopsies were performed. Cole always had a strange feeling when he came here and entered what to him looked like a hospital operating room.

Dr. Hunt stood next to a desk on one side of the room as he studied a piece of paper he held. He looked up when he heard the door open. "Cole," he called out, "come in. Glad you could make it. I wanted to give you the results of the autopsy in person." He sat down at his desk and motioned for Cole to take a chair facing him.

Cole didn't speak as the doctor let his gaze drift over the report in front of him. Then Dr. Hunt looked up, a frown on his face. "I have the results here, and I'll give you a copy for your files. After performing a thorough autopsy, I have concluded the cause of death. In fact, it's very obvious almost at first glance. The young woman died of a gunshot to the head."

Cole blinked his eyes in surprise and shook his head. "I don't understand. I was told that the doctor who signed the death certificate said it was a blood clot."

Dr. Hunt looked back at the report. "Yes, Dr. Curtis Stanford signed the death certificate. The place of death is recorded as the Wings of Hope maternity home. I understand Dr. Stanford volunteers his services to them."

Cole frowned. "If he saw the young woman's body, wouldn't he have recognized that there was a gunshot that killed her?"

"I would think so. It was very evident to me."

The muscle in Cole's jaw twitched, and he gritted his teeth. Someone had murdered Teresa Wilson and then passed it off as a result of natural causes. He thought of the twin babies she'd given birth to and wondered if she really had changed her mind and wanted them back. If so, was that why she had died? Had someone been determined to ensure she wouldn't get to keep them? For whatever reason, someone had worked to cover up her murder, and Dr. Curtis Stanford knew exactly who that was. Cole intended to find out.

Still clutching the report, he rose to his feet. "Thanks, Doc. I need to visit Dr. Stanford and see if he can explain how he made such an enormous mistake. I doubt if he has any explanation that will support what he did."

Twenty minutes later, Cole stormed into Dr. Stanford's office. On the drive over, he'd tried to calm the anger that roiled inside him. Doctors were supposed to protect their patients and care for them, not lie to cover up their murder. At best, the good doctor had made himself an accessory. There were other charges he could be facing, not the least of which was murder itself.

As he strode across the waiting room toward the receptionist, her eyes seemed to grow larger the closer he came. When he stopped in front of her desk, she almost recoiled from the anger that he was trying—and failing—to suppress.

"C-can I—I help you?" she stammered.

Cole pulled out his badge and flashed it. "Detective Cole Jackson here to see Dr. Stanford."

She raised frightened eyes and stared up at him. "Dr. Stanford is in his office doing a post-exam conference with a patient. If you'll just have a seat…"

"Never mind. I'll find my own way," he said as he marched down the hallway.

"Detective Jackson, you can't go back there!" the receptionist called after him, but he didn't acknowledge that she was speaking to him.

The doors on the left side of the hall appeared to be exam rooms, but Cole spotted one that had a nameplate identifying Dr. Stanford's office. He shoved the door open.

Dr. Stanford sat behind his desk and looked up in surprise when the door opened. He pushed to his feet, an angry frown on his face. "What do you mean interrupting me when I'm in conference? Get out of here before I call the police!"

Cole pulled his badge from his pocket. "I'm the police, and I'm already here." He glanced at the woman sitting in the guest chair. Her mouth hung open, and her eyes were wide with fear. "Ma'am," Cole said, "I think you'd better leave. Your appointment is over."

"What do you mean by barging in this way?" Dr. Stanford yelled as he rushed around his desk to confront Cole. "I'll have your job for this!"

Cole shook his head. "I don't think you'll be able to do that when you're in a cell at the state penitentiary."

Dr. Stanford stopped, and his face grew pale. "What are you talking about?"

Cole took a step forward. "I'm here to take you to the sheriff's department, so we can have a talk about a former patient of yours. Her name was Teresa Wilson. Do you remember her?" At the mention of the girl's name, the doctor's face grew even whiter. Cole chuckled. "I thought that might get your attention."

At that moment, the receptionist appeared at the door and glanced from Cole to the doctor. "Dr. Stanford, I'm so sorry. I couldn't stop him."

"It's okay," he said. "Call my lawyer and tell him to meet me at the sheriff's office."

Cole looked at the young woman and nodded. "That sounds like a good idea to me."

Then he grabbed Dr. Stanford by the arm and escorted him from the building.

The doctor didn't say anything as they rode to the sheriff's office. He continued his silence even after Cole and Dan, his partner, sat in an interview room at the sheriff's office with him and his lawyer. Ever since they'd entered the room, Dr. Stanford had sat up straight in his chair, his arms crossed in front of his chest, glaring without blinking. Even after they'd read him his rights, all the questions Cole and Dan posed had been met with an icy silence. The lawyer had been another matter, however.

He repeated again the same words that he'd uttered at the end of each question. "My client refuses to answer on the grounds it might incriminate him. Either charge him or release him."

Cole was growing tired of their stonewalling, and he was ready to bring this interview to an end. He sighed and closed the folder that lay on the table in front of him. "You're right. We either need to charge him or release him."

The lawyer grinned. "In that case, we'll be going since you haven't presented any evidence that my client was involved in anything illegal."

He started to rise from his seat, but Cole held out his hand to stop him. "We've given Dr. Stanford the chance to help us with an investigation into a young woman's death and the attempted kidnappings of two children he delivered. He may be an accessory in this case, but I'm afraid his involvement goes much deeper." He stared at Dr. Stanford. "So I'm arresting you for the murder of Teresa Wilson."

Dr. Stanford's eyes flared, and his face turned red with rage. "How dare you accuse me of something like that!"

The lawyer laid his hand on the doctor's arm and shook his head. "Nice try, Detective, but I don't think you can prove that."

Cole shrugged. "I think I have enough evidence to convince a jury. When they hear how Dr. Stanford examined a murder victim and then signed the girl's death certificate while listing cause of death as a blood clot, I think they'll convict."

A sneer pulled at the lawyer's mouth. "And everyone will believe she was murdered simply because you say so? Do you think they're going to believe your trumped-up charge against the word of a respected physician who's practiced in this community for twenty years?"

Cole folded his hands on the table and leaned forward. "I think they will. You see, we had Teresa Wilson's body exhumed. The cause of death wasn't a blood clot. It was a gunshot wound to the head. Her death certificate is an official document, and Dr. Stanford very obviously lied on it. Unless he's willing to admit to being blackmailed or bribed, then it stands to reason he's the one who murdered her and covered it up by falsifying the death certificate. Your client is looking at life in prison for murder."

Dr. Stanford and the lawyer both sat in silence for a moment. Then the doctor leaned over and whispered in his lawyer's ear. The man nodded and cleared his throat. "My client would like to make a deal. He'll give you the name of the actual killer if he can be charged with a lesser crime—perhaps falsifying a record."

Cole looked over at Dan, who shook his head. "We don't do deals. The DA's office has to decide that. But if Dr. Stanford wants to come clean now, we'll make a recommendation for a lesser charge. That's the best we can do."

The lawyer turned a questioning gaze toward Dr. Stanford, who finally took a deep breath and nodded. "Okay. I'll tell you what I know."

The doctor bit down on his lip, then began to speak. "I was the one who delivered Teresa's babies at the hospital because she'd had some problems during her pregnancy. Everything went well with the birth, and she was dismissed the next day and went back to Wings of Hope to recuperate."

Cole looked up from writing down what the doctor was saying. "Did she take the babies with her?"

He shook his head. "No, a social worker was there waiting for the babies to be born. It was my understanding that all the paperwork had been signed, and the adoptive parents were in the waiting room. As soon as the twins were pronounced healthy, the social worker took them to the new parents, and they left the hospital. When Teresa left the hospital the next day, I examined her one more time and told her I'd see her in my office in six weeks for a checkup. I didn't give her another thought until…"

"Until what?" Cole asked.

"Until I got a call from Greg Richmond to come to Wings of Hope the next day. When I got there, he took me into one of the patients' private rooms, and I saw Teresa lying on the floor. There was a pool of blood under her head. It was obvious that she'd been shot and that she was dead."

"So what did you do?"

"I told Greg we had to call the police. He said he couldn't let that happen. Teresa had decided to re-nege on the agreement to give up the babies, and she had threatened to go to the police when he told her that the adoptive parents had paid a lot of money for those babies, and he wasn't about to give it back. Teresa became hysterical because she didn't know about the money. He had forged her signature on the endorsement and deposited the money in his account. He told me that he ended up locking her in her room while he left to call a friend of his who came and took care of the situation."

"You mean he killed her?"

The doctor nodded. "That's what he told me had happened. He wanted me to sign the death certificate to say that she had died of a blood clot. I didn't want to do it at first, but Greg told me his friend was a professional hit man and he could just as easily take care of my family if I didn't cooperate." The doctor began to cry. "I have a wife and two daughters, and I knew he meant what he said. I couldn't let them be hurt, so I signed the death certificate, and he called a local funeral director who was a friend of his. Greg paid him to bury the body without any questions, and he did."

Dr. Stanford sagged back in his chair and closed his eyes. Cole stared at him for a moment before he stood and walked to the door. He opened it and spoke to the deputy who had been stationed in the hallway. "Deputy, I've placed this man under arrest. I'll need you to get him processed. Dan and I have another stop to make."

The deputy nodded and walked into the room. "Will you stand, please?"

Dr. Stanford got to his feet and winced as his hands were pulled behind his back and handcuffs were snapped in place. He looked over at his lawyer, and Cole saw the same expression in the doctor's eyes that he had seen dozens of times from people who'd participated in a crime and were beginning to see what their choice had brought them.

"Will you go see my wife and tell her what happened? Tell her I love her and that I'm sorry."

The lawyer nodded as the deputy escorted the doctor from the room. Once they were gone, the lawyer gathered up his briefcase and walked out without speaking.

Cole didn't move for a moment, just stood there thinking of how the pieces were beginning to fall into place. His and Dan's next stop might finally bring the whole affair to an ending. He certainly hoped so.

He picked up his jacket, which hung on the back

of his chair, shrugged it on and glanced at Dan. "Let's go visit Greg Richmond," he said as he headed to the door.

TWELVE

Kathy was sitting at her desk when Cole and Dan walked into the reception area at Wings of Hope. Her eyes lit up and she smiled when she saw Cole walking into the room. "Detective Jackson, it's so good to see you again."

He forced himself to smile. As angry as he was about the crime that had been committed, he knew it wasn't Kathy's fault. If she'd been involved in any way, she wouldn't have given them so much information when she'd come to Holly's house for dinner. "You, too, Kathy," he said.

"I had such a good time the other night at Miss Lee's house." A slight flush rose to her cheeks. "And I want to thank you for bringing Jason. I was so glad to meet him."

A sincere grin pulled at Cole's mouth. It was evident that the girl had a crush on their talented sketch artist. "I hope the two of you hit it off."

"Oh, we did," she gushed. "In fact, we've hung out together several times since then, and I'm going with him to Nashville this weekend so that he can audition for Keith Jefferson. He's so excited and so grateful to Miss Lee for making this possible."

The mention of Holly's name sent a jolt of remorse straight to his heart, but he didn't let it show. "Are you planning to see Holly while you're there?"

"I don't know. She may still be in Jackson Springs while we're in town."

Cole's eyebrows arched in surprise. "Still here? I thought she went back to Nashville yesterday."

Kathy shook her head. "No, she's still here. Jason talked to her last night. It seems she had a TV crew coming to do an interview today. They were going to be at her home this morning and then at the city park this afternoon."

Cole didn't say anything for a moment, and then he remembered the voice mail that he still hadn't played. Had Holly been calling to tell him she hadn't gone back to Nashville? As soon as he finished talking to Greg Richmond, he'd have to listen to it.

Pulling his thoughts away from Holly, he glanced at Dan and then back to Kathy. "This is my partner, and we'd like to speak with Mr. Richmond. Is he in?"

Kathy nodded. "He's in his office. I'll let him know you're here."

Cole held up his hand to stop her before she picked up the telephone. "Never mind. We'll announce ourselves."

A puzzled look crossed Kathy's face, and she nodded. "Okay. You know where to go."

Cole turned and headed down the hall with Dan right behind him. He paused outside Greg Richmond's office and rapped on the door.

"Come in," a muffled voice from inside called out.

Cole opened the door and stepped into the room with Dan right behind. Richmond looked up, a startled expression on his face when he saw them entering. "Detective Jackson, come in. To what do I owe this pleasure?"

On the way to Wings of Hope, he and Dan had decided that they would hit Richmond right away with the reason for their visit, in the hopes of getting an unguarded reaction before the man had a chance to hide his response. "We're here to arrest you for the murder of Teresa Wilson."

Richmond's mouth gaped open, and he stared at them from where he sat behind his desk. The look on his face told Cole the man couldn't believe what he was hearing. A choking sound came from his throat as his terrified gaze flitted from Cole to Dan. "Are you out of your mind? Teresa died of a blood clot."

Cole shook his head. "It's too late for that argument, Richmond. An autopsy revealed that she died of a gunshot wound, and your friend Dr. Stanford is at the station now telling his side of the story. We're ready to hear yours. Things will go a lot easier on you if you give us the name of your friend who murdered Teresa. I have a feeling, though, that the name you'll tell us is Willie Trask. Is that right?"

A sneer pulled at Richmond's mouth. "I don't know what you're talking about."

"We'll see," Cole said. He took a step toward Richmond and began to read him his rights. When he was finished, he motioned toward the door. "Come on. Let's go."

Richmond sat still for a moment and then began to rise slowly. As he did, his hand drifted down to the desk drawer on his right. Before Cole knew what had happened, he'd whipped out a gun and aimed it at them. "I'm not going anywhere with you."

Dan and Cole moved away from each other, to create some distance between them. Richmond moved the gun back and forth between them as if unsure of which one to shoot at first. "Put the gun down," Cole ordered. "We don't want anybody to get hurt here today."

"Nobody will if you stay out of my way."

He slowly moved out from behind the desk and took a step toward Cole. He jerked his head in the direction of Dan. "Get over there by your partner." When Cole didn't move, he yelled, "Now!"

Cole took a step toward Dan but kept his eyes trained on Richmond. "You can't get away with this. If you leave here, the authorities will have an alert out for you before you can get out of town. There won't be anywhere you can run that we won't find you."

Richmond chuckled. "That's going to be hard to do."

Cole frowned. What was he talking about? Before he could ask the question, though, he saw Dan make a move to pull his gun from his holster. He had just pulled it clear when a shot rang out. The gun dropped from Dan's hand, and his body jerked once as he slumped to the floor.

Cole caught sight of the gun on the floor and dived for it before Richmond could get off another shot. He grabbed the gun and lunged to his feet, the weapon pointed at Richmond. "Drop your gun or I'll shoot."

Richmond laughed and shook his head. "I don't think so. I'm going…"

Before he could finish what he was about to say, the office door burst open, and Kathy rushed into the room. At the sight of her boss and Cole in a stand-off, she came to a stop. When she spotted Dan on the floor, she turned a frightened look back to Richmond and started to run, but she wasn't fast enough.

Richmond grabbed her around the waist, pulled her against him so that her back was against his front, and pointed the gun at her head. "Drop your weapon, Detective, or I'll blow her brains out."

Kathy's face turned pale, and Cole was afraid she might faint any minute. "There's no need to add more charges on top of what we already have. Let the girl go."

Richmond shook his head. "Not a chance." He pressed the gun harder against her temple and glared at Cole. "What's it going to be?"

Cole knew there was only one thing to do. Carefully, he laid the gun down. "There. I've done as you asked. Now let her go."

"Not just yet." He eased over to his desk and picked up a key ring that lay there. "Kathy and I are leaving. We're going to lock the door on our way out. If you want her to live, you'll not try to stop me." He moved toward the doorway, the key ring he'd picked up off the desk dangling in the hand around Kathy's waist. "Take the key out of my hand, Kathy. When we're in the hallway, lock these nice detectives in here."

The frightened girl nodded and reached for the keys. Cole took a step toward him. "Let Kathy go now. You're not going to get far, Richmond."

He just laughed and tugged Kathy closer. Suddenly, Kathy's arm arced up, and she stabbed the keys into Richmond's face. He howled in pain and released her. As she fell to the floor, Cole knew he had no more than a second to take his shot. Training kicked in, and he aimed at center mass, just as he'd been taught, before firing. The blast knocked Richmond into the hall, where he fell and lay still.

Cole was on him in a minute and took away his gun. Richmond didn't move as Cole examined the chest wound that was pumping blood onto the floor. He felt for a pulse and then pulled his jacket off and pressed it against Richmond's chest. Kathy stood in the office doorway, her eyes wide as she stared at Richmond and then back to Dan. She looked like she might go into shock, so he gave her something to focus on. "How's Dan? Check on him for me, will you?"

She rushed to obey his instruction. "His shoulder is bleeding, but his pulse is strong."

"Okay. Now, I need you to call nine-one-one. Tell them we have an officer and a suspect down."

Kathy turned and ran back to the phone at the desk. He could hear her talking to the dispatcher, and then she reappeared at the door. "They're on their way."

"Good," he said. His partner needed help, but it looked like Richmond was the critical one. He couldn't let the man die. Not until he'd told them who had killed Teresa and why the twins were in danger. He put Kathy to work applying pressure on Dan's injury while he stayed with Richmond.

He pressed harder against the wound and waited for the sound of sirens.

* * *

Holly propped her hands on her hips and concentrated for a moment, trying to decide if she had everything she'd need for their short trip to the park. It seemed like every time she left the house she was packing for an extended stay somewhere. She would never have believed how many necessary items were needed to cover whatever might occur.

Today, she'd packed a bag with apple juice, sippy cups, crackers, sunscreen, extra outfits in case Emma and Ethan got their clothes dirty, Ziploc bags for soiled diapers, a blanket for each of them in case they got chilly and bottled water. Then there was the diaper bag that contained a changing pad, diapers, teething gel because they were cutting their first molars and antibacterial wipes.

Satisfied that she had everything, she looked around for her purse and cringed at the idea that she'd have one more thing to keep up with. Since Mandy was busy interviewing applicants for the nanny position and working on publicity for the upcoming tour and with Mrs. Green leaving shortly for a dentist appointment, it would just be Todd and Ray with her this afternoon. They'd be focused on keeping them safe, and she couldn't expect them to carry bags around for her as well.

After a moment, she decided there was no need for a purse, but she did want her cell phone. She pulled it from her purse, put it on vibrate in case it rang during the interview and stuck it down in the diaper bag. Satisfied that she had everything, she picked up the bags, called out to Mandy that she was ready to leave and carried all her supplies to the car.

Todd and Ray were waiting for them. "Did you put the stroller in the back?" Holly asked as she stuck the bags inside the trunk.

"Yes, ma'am. That's all taken care of."

The front door of the house opened and Mandy and Mrs. Green emerged, each holding one of the babies. The twins began to smile and kick their legs in excitement when they saw her standing by the car. Holly's heart warmed at the thought that they knew they were about to go for a ride with their aunt.

She took Emma in her arms and buckled her in one of the car seats while Todd carried Ethan around the side of the car and fastened him in the other. When they were both secure, Holly turned back to the women whom she'd come to depend on so much. "Thank you for all your help. I hope your dental appointment isn't too painful, Mrs. Green, and I'll check with you on your progress when I get back, Mandy."

Both women stepped away from the vehicle and waved at the children as Holly climbed in the car and settled herself between the two babies. Ray glanced over his shoulder to make sure they were secure and then guided the SUV out of the driveway. As they rode toward the park, a tingle of apprehension ran through her body. Hopefully, the filming would go quickly. She didn't really feel comfortable about being out in the open park with the twins this afternoon.

It only took a few minutes to get to their destination, and when they approached, she sighted a barricade across the entrance to the park. A man in a uniform that identified him as a park employee stood there. Ray pulled to a stop and spoke a few words to the man, who nodded and then opened the barricade.

As they entered, Holly glanced around. She had come to this park so many times with her sister when they were growing up and with Cole when they were dating. There were a lot of memories here, but today she had a growing concern that she shouldn't be there. She looked around as Ray pulled the car to a stop.

"Do you think we're going to be safe, Todd?"

"I do, Miss Lee. Ray and I will make sure of it."

Satisfied with his answer, she climbed out when he opened the door and waited for Ray to bring the stroller from the back. Emma and Ethan squealed in glee as she and Todd picked them up and deposited them in the two seats. She hung her bags over the handle and smiled at how excited they were to be outside.

The camera crew was already there, and she pushed the twins to where Stephen and Mark, the cameramen from earlier, stood. "I have everything ready, Miss Lee. I don't want you to have to keep your children out here longer than needed. I'm going to do some shots of you playing with the babies until the Davenports get here. Then you can concentrate on the interview."

"That sounds great, Stephen. The sun's rather hot today, and I don't want to take a chance on them getting sunburned."

"Why don't you spread a blanket and sit down with them while I'm getting my camera ready? Just relax and make this look like a typical trip to the park with your children."

Typical? The word echoed in her head. There was

nothing typical in her life, not since she'd left Jackson Springs. That thought brought Cole to mind, and her heart pricked at the silence she'd gotten in response to her voice mail. He'd had plenty of time to call her if he had wanted to, so all she could conclude was that he wasn't interested in what she had to say. She blinked back tears as she settled the twins on the blanket and sank down beside them with the sunscreen.

Stephen came back with the camera just then, and all thoughts of Cole fled from her mind as she concentrated on corralling the twins in one area and making it look like a *typical* afternoon at the park. As she slathered the sunscreen on the two active babies, she became so engrossed in her task that she didn't hear the car at first.

Suddenly Todd's voice roared through the air. "Get down!"

Holly looked up and stared in shock at an SUV speeding across the grass toward them. She put her arms around the babies and started to gather them up to run away from the oncoming danger, but then the vehicle came to a stop and two men jumped out.

Todd whipped out his gun, but before he could pull the trigger, one of the men fired and Todd slumped to the ground. The other man had a gun aimed at Ray, and its blast echoed through the park.

Holly screamed as the two men advanced toward her. Stephen, the cameraman, tried to approach, but a bullet cut him down before he could reach her. He fell to the ground, his camera beside him. Stephen's assistant, Mark, sprinted away from them as bullets flew through the air all around him. She hoped he had made it safely away to call for help.

The two men who'd climbed out of the car walked up to her, and one of them spoke in a calm voice. "Miss Lee, I want you to pick up one of the twins. I'll get the other while my friend here keeps a gun trained on you. If you try anything foolish, he will kill you. Do you understand?"

Her voice wouldn't make a sound, so she nodded.

"Good," he said. "Let's go."

Holly rose to her feet and grabbed Ethan while the man picked up Emma. They started toward the car, and she spotted the bags still hanging on the stroller handle. "Please, we need those bags for the children."

He frowned as if he wasn't going to heed her request but then reached out and slung the bags over his shoulder. The other man holding the gun nudged her forward, and she swallowed down the fear that clogged her throat. Who were these men and where were they taking them? And most important, would she and the twins survive once they got there?

Cole paced the hospital's ER reception area as he waited for the doctor to come talk to him about Dan's condition. The room was packed with Dan's family members, all except his wife, who had followed a nurse from the room a few minutes earlier. Deputies, some on duty and in uniform while others wore civilian clothes, stood about, having come in on their day off. All were there to support a brother who had fallen today in the line of duty. He groaned as he raked his hand through his hair and turned to trace the path he'd followed across the floor for the last hour, praying for his friend's condition. What was taking so long?

The door to the exam rooms in the back opened,

and the doctor walked out. He looked around, and then his eyes landed on Cole. "Are you Detective Welch's partner?"

Cole swallowed. "I am. How is he?"

A smile spread across his face. "He's going to be fine. The bullet passed through his shoulder but didn't do any major internal damage. He'll be off work for a while, but he should recover completely. The other man didn't fare so well. He suffered a severe chest wound, and he's been sent to ICU."

Cole let out a huge sigh of relief at the news about Dan. He was also glad Greg Richmond had survived so far. He had questions to answer. "Thank you, Doctor. When can I speak to Greg Richmond?"

The doctor shook his head. "I'm afraid it's going to be a while. He's heavily sedated and on a respirator. He won't be able to talk for days."

Cole nodded and tried to keep the disappointment that he wouldn't be allowed in yet from showing on his face. "I'll keep checking on him and come back when you say it's all right. In the meantime, can I see Dan?"

"Sure. I'll take you back myself. His wife's with him right now, but he'll be glad to see you."

Cole followed the doctor back to Dan's hospital room and fifteen minutes later emerged satisfied that Dan was going to be all right. He felt as if a great burden had been lifted from his shoulders as he walked from the hospital toward his car. When he climbed in, he was about to start the engine when he thought of Holly's message again. He had never listened to it.

He pulled his phone from his pocket and stared at it before he punched the button to connect to his voice mail. His skin warmed as the sound of her voice rippled in his ear: "Cole, this is Holly."

As he sat there in shock, he heard what Holly was saying, but he almost couldn't believe it was true. Cole sat there for several minutes as he tried to digest what he'd just heard. Holly loved him, and she wanted to stay in Jackson Springs. The questions began to fly through his mind. How could they reconcile their two lives? What if she decided she wanted to leave again? Could he risk going through the heartbreak a second time?

He bowed his head and poured out his heart to God. "I love her so much, God, and I want to be with her, but I'm scared. Help me find the answer to what I should do."

He sat there for a while before he opened his eyes. A new certainty filled him. There was only one thing to do. Put his trust in God that He would be there for him no matter what happened. If the two of them still loved each other, God could work out all the problems.

With a heart lighter than it had been in years, he reached for the ignition. Before he could turn the key, his cell phone chimed with the station's ringtone. He connected the call. "Hello."

"Cole, this is Brenda. I thought I'd better call you and tell you what happened."

Her voice was shaking, and Cole sat up straighter in the seat. "What is it, Brenda?"

"Holly Lee was doing an interview in the city park with her two children when a car broke through the barricade her security team had erected and barreled right to her." She stopped, and a sob reached his ear.

Cole's heart was in his throat. "Brenda! Tell me what happened!"

"Two men shot both her security team members and one of the cameramen. His assistant got away and called the police."

"And Holly? What happened to her?"

"They abducted her and the children."

He felt as if the life had just left his body. Just minutes ago, he'd been ready to run to Holly and tell her how much he loved her, too. Now she was missing, along with Emma and Ethan. Despair washed over him, and he covered his eyes with his hand. He had to do something to get them back. But what?

"Brenda," he said, "I'm on my way to the park."

"There's no need for that. The police are already there, and the three men who were shot are en route to the hospital."

"What's their conditions?"

"I don't know, but maybe one of them can talk."

"Thanks, Brenda. I'll stay in touch."

He disconnected the call and sat staring out the windshield. He couldn't lose Holly. Not when they were so close to being happy together. At the moment, though, he had no idea which way to turn. Maybe one of the injured men would be able to tell him something to help him go in the right direction.

The sound of an ambulance's siren pulled him from his thoughts, and he watched as the emergency vehicle pulled into the parking lot and backed up to the unloading bay. Several nurses and orderlies rushed out the door as the paramedics jumped from the vehicle.

Cole took a deep breath, got out of his car and

walked back toward the emergency room. As he headed into the reception area, he said a quick prayer that these men would survive and would give him some information that would help him find the woman he loved and the children he wanted to raise with her.

THIRTEEN

Emma and Ethan weren't doing well in the strange car seats they'd been buckled into. It was as if they sensed danger, and they had been crying ever since their abductors had driven away from the park. She had done everything she could think of to soothe them, but nothing was working.

The man who'd shot Todd looked over his shoulder at her and glared. "Keep those kids quiet, or I'll shut them up myself."

The tone of his voice sent fear spiraling through her, and she leaned over and kissed Emma's tiny hands that reached for her. The crying only ramped up in volume when she didn't pull Emma from the car seat. Holly tried to ignore the panic that was building inside her. She'd never felt so helpless in her life. She had to do something, but she didn't know what.

"Why are you doing this?" she asked the man in front of her.

He glanced back at her and grinned maliciously. "Why does anybody do anything? For money. I'm getting paid very well for this."

"For abducting my children?" she yelled. "What kind of man are you?"

"I'm one who finishes every job I start, and I intend to finish this one."

"But why?" Holly begged. "We've done nothing to you. Why would you want to hurt these babies?"

He chuckled, and the sound of it made Holly's skin crawl. "I don't want to hurt them. I panicked at the supermarket when I pushed them in front of that car. At the time I was only concerned with getting away. But you don't have to worry now. I'll take good care of them. They're worth a lot of money to me. You, on the other hand, aren't, so you might want to shut up before you make me angry."

His words made no sense to Holly. She knew she should be quiet, but she couldn't refrain from speaking. "Do you want money? I have lots of money. I'll pay you whatever you want to let us go. I promise I won't say anything to the police."

"Well, you see, that sounds good, but I know you won't keep your word. You'll head straight to the cops, and they'll be after me in no time. This way, I can get my money and be on my way without anybody knowing Willie Trask was involved."

A chill ran through Holly, and she gaped at the man. "You're Willie Trask, the man Sarah Palmer warned us about?"

He shook his head and pursed his lips. "Poor Sarah. She should have kept her mouth shut. Maybe if she had, she'd still be alive. So would Teresa Wilson if she'd just let the twins go."

The mention of Teresa jolted Holly to attention. She sucked in a quick breath. "Did you kill Teresa?"

"She had it coming. She shouldn't have backed out of the deal."

Holly had suspected that Teresa had been killed—that was why Cole had gotten a court order for the autopsy, after all—but it was still a shock to hear the man admit it so casually. She stared in disbelief at Willie. "You killed her because she'd decided not to give up the twins."

Willie swiveled in his seat and stared at her with burning eyes. "Yeah. That meant the money we'd gotten from your sister and brother-in-law would have to be returned, and we ran the risk of their telling the police about how we'd sold them two babies. There was nothing else we could do. She had to be stopped."

Tears burned Holly's eyes as she stared at Emma and Ethan. Her heart broke for the young woman who'd decided she couldn't give up her babies, for her sister and brother-in-law, who had gotten in the middle of a baby-selling operation, and for the twins she'd come to love, who would never know any of the first three parents to love them.

"You're despicable," she muttered. "I'll see that you are punished for what you've done."

He laughed and shook his head. "I doubt that. I don't think you'll survive long enough to tell anybody."

"I don't understand," she said. "Why didn't you just kill me at the park if you only wanted the children?"

Willie shrugged. "I just follow orders, and I was told to bring you with us."

Her heart pounded so hard she was afraid he might hear it. "But you won't hurt the children?"

"No. The new buyer might not like getting damaged goods."

Holly could only stare in disbelief. "You're selling them to someone else?" she screeched.

He shrugged. "Well, I'm not. But Greg is. He's supposed to meet us."

"Wh-where is he sending them?"

"Somewhere they'll never be found."

Holly leaned back in the seat, unable to bring herself to ask anything more. Thankfully, the twins had finally settled down. She dozed off but woke when the car hit something that made it jerk. She opened her eyes and stared out the window as she tried to figure out where she was. They passed a road that turned off to the right, and she recognized it as one that led to the top of a mountain she and Cole had hiked many times.

She frowned and glanced around as a run-down cabin with a helicopter pad beside it came into view. She recognized it right away. Mo Calloway had lived there for years and had run helicopter flights for tourists over the mountains until his death. No one had lived there since, as far as she knew. She looked around for other cars, but there were none in sight. Then her gaze drifted back to the helicopter pad, and she remembered what Trask had said about his and Greg's plans for the children. A sick feeling began to gnaw at her stomach, and she swallowed the bile that flowed into her mouth.

She wished this was a horrible nightmare that she could wake up from, but she knew it wasn't. She was about to die, and Emma and Ethan were about to disappear into the dark world of child trafficking.

* * *

Cole paced up and down the hospital waiting-room floor just as he had done earlier when Dan and Greg had been brought in. Now the reason he couldn't sit still was because he needed to talk to the survivors from the shooting in the park. He just hoped someone had noticed a hint or a clue that would lead him to where the abductors had taken Holly and the children.

He stopped in his tracks when the door to the emergency wing swung open and the same doctor he'd talked with earlier emerged. He headed straight to Cole.

"You're back again?"

"Yeah, Doc. Tell me how the victims of the park shooting are doing."

The doctor sighed and rubbed his eyes. "It's touch and go with the two men who were working security. If they make it through the night, they have a chance. The wounded cameraman is in better condition. The bullet that hit him grazed his head, but didn't penetrate to do any serious damage. There was a lot of blood. That's probably what saved his life. He pretended to be unconscious, and the attackers saw the blood and thought he was dead. They might have finished him off if they'd known he was faking."

"I'm glad he was able to think that quickly. So you think he'll be okay?"

"He should be," the doctor said. "He's awake and is asking to see the investigator in charge of the case. Is that you?"

Cole rubbed the back of his neck and nodded. "I

guess that's me. Both shootings are linked. If I solve one, the other one will fall into place."

"Well, follow me, and I'll show you where he is."

Just as he had done earlier, Cole followed the doctor down the hallway to one of the hospital rooms. When they stopped, the doctor pointed to the door. "He's in there. Don't wear him out."

"I won't, Doc. Thanks."

Cole tapped on the door, and a voice from inside called out. "Come in."

He opened the door and stepped inside. A young man who appeared to be in his late twenties lay on the bed. The bandage covered most of his forehead, and he stared at Cole with dark eyes. "I understand you were the cameraman with Holly Lee at the park."

He nodded. "Yes. My name is Stephen Blakemore."

Cole stepped over to the bed. "I'm Detective Cole Jackson. I'm here to ask you some questions about the abduction. Do you feel up to talking?"

He nodded. "Yes. I want to do everything I can to help Miss Lee and those babies."

Cole pulled out his notepad. "Tell me what you were doing with Miss Lee today."

He took notes as Stephen told him about the interview, how they'd worked at her house in the morning and then gone to the park to document an outing with the twins. "Everything was going fine until this SUV roared up and bullets began to fly."

Cole looked up and pointed his pen at Stephen's head. "The doctor says you were smart enough to fool them."

Stephen chuckled. "For some reason, I knew I needed to lie still. I guess they thought I was dead."

"Had you ever seen either of the men before?"

"No. But I won't forget what they looked like."

Cole nodded. "I guess going through something like that would leave an impression on your mind. We have a sketch artist at the station who is very good. If I had him come over, do you think you could describe the men?"

Stephen frowned and shook his head. "There's no need for that. I can just give you the video, and you can see for yourself."

"What do you mean?" Cole asked.

Stephen pushed himself up in the bed and pointed to his camera that lay on a chair across the room. "I had my camera rolling when they drove up. I turned around and aimed the camera at them. That's when they shot me."

Cole's heartbeat quickened as he stared at the camera. "Do you think you caught them on the video?"

Stephen laughed. "I did better than catch them. I kept the camera rolling all the time I was on the ground, and I filmed the whole abduction. Even got the car and the license plate when they drove away."

Cole could hardly believe what he'd just heard. "You got the SUV's license number?"

"Yeah. Want me to show you?"

Cole strode over to the chair, grabbed the camera and handed it to Stephen. "Show me what you have."

The video only lasted a few minutes, but Cole didn't think he'd ever seen anything that tore his heart out like that short clip. The scene was filled with joy when it opened with Holly and the twins sitting on a blanket in the park, but it quickly turned to terror with the roar of a speeding vehicle. He flinched when Todd, Ray and Stephen were shot and then bit down on his quivering lip as he saw Holly and the children pulled into the SUV. As the vehicle pulled away, the camera zoomed in on the license plate, displaying it in perfect clarity just as Stephen had said.

Cole grabbed his cell phone and hit speed dial for the office line. Brenda answered on the first ring. "Cole, is that you?"

"Yes. I'm at the hospital. The cameraman got a shot of the abductor's license plate. Let me read it to you." He rattled off the number and then paused. "Did you get that?"

"Got it."

"Put out a BOLO on it right away, and check the DMV records for the registration. I'm on my way to the station, but call me as soon as you've ID'd the owner."

"Will do," she said before hanging up.

Cole exhaled a deep breath and reached out to shake hands with Stephen. "Good work, Stephen. You've helped us a lot, and I hope you don't have to stay here too long."

The young man grinned. "I hope so, too, and I'll be praying you find Miss Lee and those two children."

"Thanks. That's all we've got going for us right now, but as the Bible says, 'If God be for us, who can be against us?'"

With a wave, Cole headed to the door and out to the parking lot. He'd just gotten in his car when his cell phone rang. It was the department.

"Brenda, what do you have for me?"

"The car belongs to a rental agency out of Knoxville. They say the car was rented yesterday by a man named Willie Trask. When we ran his name earlier, we found out he has a record for everything from armed robbery to assault. He's had several murder accusations, but nothing could ever be proved."

"Thanks, Brenda. I'm coming back to the station right now." He started to disconnect the call, but a sudden thought struck him. "Brenda, are you still there?"

"I am."

"I was just thinking. Holly never goes anywhere without her cell phone. Tell our tech guys to see if they can track the location and any movement on it."

"Will do," she said and then hung up.

Cole stared out the window for several minutes and thought back over the video he'd just seen. He mentally replayed it from beginning to end, but he couldn't figure out anything that would help him locate where the men had taken Holly and the twins.

His heart ached at the thought of how scared she must be right now. He had to find her. He could only hope that she had her cell phone, and that her captors hadn't taken it away. If it was still with her, they might be able to locate where they'd been taken.

He cranked the engine and put the car in gear. "Hang on, Holly, and don't give up. I'm coming for you and the twins."

The twins had quieted during the drive, but now that they were waiting at the cabin, their fussing had started up again. Holly had tried everything she knew to quiet Emma and Ethan, but nothing had worked. Trask had brought them inside the cabin in their car seats and ordered her to leave them buckled up. They were furious at being imprisoned, and they'd screamed in anger ever since. She'd fed them, played peekaboo until she thought she would go crazy and begged them to settle down.

Now she was singing to them. She'd spent many hours with them in the nursery, singing them to sleep, since they'd been with her, and it had become a favorite activity for her. It sliced her heart in two as she thought this might be the last time she'd get to do it.

She sang one lullaby after another and watched with satisfaction as the cries tapered down and their eyes began to droop. When they drifted off, she pulled their blankets out of the bag and covered each of them. She watched them as they slept and thought again of Ruth and Michael, and how they had loved these children.

Trask sat at a table across the room, and he stared at her as she walked over to where he was sitting. "Did you kill my sister and brother-in-law?"

He laughed and shook his head. "You sure ask a lot of questions."

"If I'm going to die today, I want to know before I do. Did you kill them?"

He studied her for a moment. "Yeah. I had a friend who worked at the airfield where they'd landed their plane in New Orleans. He distracted them while I slipped something in Michael's coffee before they took off. It was a drug to make him fall asleep while flying."

Tears burned her eyes. "I don't understand why you did it."

Willie pushed to his feet and stalked over to where she stood. He glared down at her and growled, "I'm tired of your questions."

"I'll quit asking them when I get some answers."

Willie stared at her for a moment and then shrugged. "It was simple. Some rich hotshot wanted year-old twins. Seems like his, a boy and a girl, were killed in a car wreck, and his wife was grieving herself to death. He offered a lot of money to Wings of Hope if they could get him a replacement set. The only ones that had been born there were with your sister and brother-in-law. Greg knew they'd never give them up, and he didn't have time to find others. He didn't think you'd want to give them up either, so he decided on kidnapping them."

"I would never have let them go," Holly hissed.

Willie sighed. "Yeah, I know. So we had to change our plans."

"You're disgusting!" Holly hissed. "How could you think I would ever want to benefit from the loss of the only members of my family I had left?"

"It doesn't matter now. Everything's going to work out fine. We have the babies, and we'll be paid well. With you out of the way, there won't be any family to push for the case to remain active. After a while it'll go cold. We'll all live happily ever after."

"I'm warning you. You won't get away with this."

Willie started to reply, but a sound from outside stopped him. He grinned at Holly as the sound grew louder, and she frowned as she identified the noise as a helicopter landing.

Willie shook his head and laughed. "Looks like we've *already* gotten away with it. I was just waiting for Greg so we could take off, and it looks like he just arrived."

"He's not coming," a voice said from the direction of the door.

Holly turned slowly and gasped at the sight of Julie Swanson standing in the open door. "Greg got himself shot this afternoon," she said. "So I'm taking over now, and I don't intend for there to be any more mistakes."

FOURTEEN

Cole jumped from his car and ran in the front door of the sheriff's office. Several deputies stood in the hall, and Brenda rose from her desk as he came in. "Cole," she called out. "The tech guys want you in their office right away."

He didn't stop, just nodded and ran down the hall. When he got to the room, he burst in and found the two tech workers hovered over a computer. They looked up, and one motioned for him to come over. "I think we found them," he said.

He pointed to the computer screen, where a small red triangle showed up. "Where is that?" Cole asked.

"It's a road that turns off Highway 66 near Sevierville. We tracked the phone, and it came to a stop here just before you came in. Do you know this area?"

Cole scanned the screen as he tried to visualize the location. Suddenly, he knew where they were headed. Mo Calloway's old helicopter site. That was the only place in that remote area.

"I know where this is!" Cole shouted. "It's a deserted helicopter site." He turned and headed for the door. "Pin down the exact address and get a SWAT team on the way up there. I'm heading there now."

Without waiting for a reply, Cole took off at a run for the parking lot. He jumped in his car and peeled out onto the street. If Holly's abductors were planning on leaving by helicopter, he didn't have any time to waste. It had already been long enough since she and the twins were taken that they could already be long gone. There was no time to waste.

He pressed his foot harder on the accelerator, and his car lurched forward. As he sped along the highway, he kept a lookout in his rearview mirror for the SWAT team. They shouldn't be too far behind him since they were always ready to deploy within minutes of getting an order. Just before he turned off the highway, he caught sight of a van barreling down behind him. His reinforcements had arrived.

Just seeing their vehicle gave him a new boost of confidence, and he said another prayer that they would arrive in time to help Holly and the twins. He couldn't lose her now. They'd been through too much and come so far since she'd arrived home. The fear that the happiness they wanted was slipping through his fingers hit him like a punch in the stomach. He had to get to her in time.

The turnoff for the road to Mo's cabin came into sight, and he turned his signal light on so the driver behind would know where they were going. He slowed some but still the car felt as if it took the turn on two tires. He tightened his grip on the steering wheel and guided the car back onto its side of the two-lane road that stretched before him.

Suddenly, a whirring sound filled the air. He stared

upward as a sleek helicopter passed overhead and flew in the same direction they were heading. The sight gave him renewed hope. If they were planning to transport Holly and the twins by helicopter, it was just arriving at the cabin. They weren't too late.

Cole kept his eyes on the helicopter's blinking lights as he followed its path down the road. When it began to descend, he realized they were about a quarter of a mile from the house. He pulled over and jumped from his car.

The van came to a stop behind him, and the doors burst open. Seven SWAT team members piled out onto the road. Even though they were dressed in full body armor and carried ballistic shields and assault rifles, he recognized their leader, Bruce Ivey, right away. They'd worked together on other hostage situations.

Bruce trotted over to him and stopped. "Tell me what we're facing here."

"I'm not sure. I know at least two gunmen are inside the cabin, but a helicopter just landed. There may be more armed assailants on board. These people are holding a woman and two babies hostage in the cabin. I think they may be getting ready to transport them."

Bruce nodded and called for one of his men, who jogged up with a motion detector in his hand. "Move in on the house and monitor the inside for movement. We'll get in place and be ready when you give the signal that someone's exiting."

The man nodded and moved off through the late-afternoon shadows.

Quietly, Cole and the rest of the SWAT team headed toward the house but spread out in different directions as it came into sight. Two skirted the cabin to take up their posts at the back door while Cole, along with Bruce and his two sharpshooters, fanned out across the front.

The SUV that Cole had seen on Stephen's video was parked beside the cabin, and a helicopter sat on Mo's old landing pad, its rotors still turning. As Cole watched, the door of the helicopter opened, and two men stepped out. He couldn't make out who they were at this distance but continued to watch as one of them reached back inside and helped someone else to the ground.

A gasp escaped his throat as he recognized the figure walking toward the house: Julie Swanson. For a moment, he just stared at her in disbelief. Yes, he'd been suspicious about the display of wealth from her clothes to her travel portfolio, but he'd never suspected that she'd be involved in something like this. He watched as she and the men walked into the cabin and shut the door.

It seemed the perpetrators he'd been looking for had just all assembled in the cabin, and he and the SWAT team had to take them down. And they had to do it without injuring Holly or Emma and Ethan. The problem was he had no clue how they were going to do that.

Holly looked at Julie Swanson, unable to believe her eyes. "You?" she gasped. "What are you doing here?"

Julie sighed and glanced over at Willie. "I'm here to try and straighten out the mess that Willie and Greg have made of this whole situation."

A small hope flared in Holly. "Does that mean you're going to let us go?"

Julie frowned and shook her head. "I'm afraid that isn't an option. All I can do now is try to make sure the rest of their plan goes off without any more hitches."

"What do you mean? And how are you involved in all of this?"

Julie sighed. "I suppose it won't hurt to tell you now since you won't be repeating what I say. Several years ago, I had a client come to me wanting to do a private adoption. They'd been turned down by all the agencies they had applied to and had decided that maybe they could pay a mother to give up her baby. They wanted me to find a child for them."

Holly could already see where this story was going. "So you went to Greg Richmond. He had babies. Instead of letting them be adopted through the state agency, you and he could arrange private adoptions and receive a lot of money from the adoptive parents."

Julie smiled. "You're smart, Holly. That's exactly what we did, and you're right—we made a lot of money at it." Her eyes suddenly glowed, and she leaned forward. "A lot of money. For the first time in his life, Greg had money to do the things he wanted to do, and I had money to travel like I'd always wanted."

"The pictures in your office," Holly gasped. "You traveled to all those places with the money you got for selling babies. One thing I don't understand, though. How much did the mothers get for giving up their babies?"

Julie laughed. "Nothing at all. I was always quick

to inform them of the things adoptive parents could provide and then tell them that it is illegal to accept payment for giving up their baby. When the parents gave us a check for the mother, it was simple to endorse it with a forged signature and transfer the funds to an offshore account. That way Greg and I could split everything the adoptive parents paid us."

"That's horrible," Holly exclaimed.

Julie shrugged. "It didn't hurt anybody until I had a client in Europe who offered a small fortune for a set of twins. When I told Greg about it, he wanted to follow through on the request right away. Since he didn't have any expectant mothers with twins, he decided to try to get your sister's babies back. I told him we'd just have to look for a mother with twins. But he didn't listen to me. He and Willie concocted this crazy scheme to get the babies, and that's brought us here today. Greg's in the hospital under arrest, and I've had to scurry to get money transferred so I can leave the country before the cops come knocking at my door."

Holly's stomach clenched at the unconcerned way Julie revealed what had led to this moment. She didn't sound as if she'd wanted Ruth and Michael to die—but she didn't seem especially upset about it, either. All that mattered to her was that she got her money. Holly shook her head. "I can't believe that you, a trusted lawyer, could get mixed up in something like this. You won't get away with it, you know. Cole will never stop looking for me or for the twins."

"Well, he can look all he wants, but there won't be anything to find. The babies are going to be hidden behind the walls of a wealthy estate in Europe. I'm going to be living on an island in the South Seas, and you are going to be resting atop a mountain in the Smokies."

Holly's eyes grew wide, and she tried to protest but no sound came from her mouth. She shook her head and took a step back from Julie.

Julie turned to Willie. "Get them all in the helicopter. When we get over one of the remotest peaks, throw Holly out. Her body won't be found there."

Willie grinned. "You got it."

Julie glared at him. "Don't think I'm through with you. We've got a lot of talking to do when this is all over about the ways you messed things up." Willie didn't respond, and Julie turned to the other two men in the room. "Get these babies aboard, and, Willie, you bring Holly."

The men walked over and each picked up a car seat that the babies were still buckled into. She didn't know how they'd slept through all that had been happening in the cabin in the last few minutes, but they had. With the sudden movement of being carried, though, they both jerked awake and howled in protest. Holly took a step toward them, but Willie grabbed her arm and pulled her back.

"No!" he said and slapped her across the face.

She let out a piercing scream as the blow knocked her to the floor. Willie reached down and jerked her to her feet. "Let's go. It's time you went for a ride."

Holly thought she was going to pass out as she watched the men holding the twins open the door and step outside with them. She took a deep breath and screamed again, but they were already out of view.

* * *

Cole watched the cabin and debated on the best way to get into the cabin. The SWAT team could easily break the door down and be inside within seconds, but that would give the abductors time to react. Which could prove deadly for Holly and the babies.

Bruce crawled over next to where Cole lay and whispered, "I have my best sniper stationed to take out anybody coming through the front door. Do you want to wait or let us go in?"

Cole closed his eyes for a moment and tried to decide what the best course of action was. A sudden scream from inside the cabin jerked him from his thoughts, and he stiffened. That was Holly's voice. Had they hurt her or one of the babies?

"Let's go!" he hissed at Bruce and jumped to his feet.

Before they could move, the door opened and two men emerged from the cabin. Each of them carried a car seat with one of the twins sitting in it. The babies were howling at the top of their lungs, and he could hear Holly's voice pleading for them not to take her babies.

Cole's heart dropped to the pit of his stomach at the pitiful sounds coming from all three of them. He started to surge forward, but before he could, two shots rang out. The men carrying the babies released their grips and fell to the ground.

Two of the SWAT team members emerged from behind some trees to his left and raced across the yard. They scooped up the babies and disappeared back into the tree line. Cole breathed a sigh of relief that Emma and Ethan were safe, but Holly was still inside.

"We're the police!" Cole shouted. "Come out with your hands in the air."

"I don't think so," a voice yelled back. "If you take one step toward us, the world will be short one country-music star."

"You can't get away!" Cole yelled back. "You need to give up while you still can."

"I don't think so," the man said. "We're going to walk out of here to the helicopter. Your girlfriend is going with us as insurance that you won't do anything."

"I don't think so. You'll kill her anyway if I let you leave."

"That's a chance you'll have to take."

Cole hesitated before answering. He turned to Bruce. "Are your guys still in place behind the cabin?"

Bruce nodded. "I can send them in the back, and we'll rush the front. That may be our best option for getting Miss Lee out alive."

Cole closed his eyes. What should he do? If they rushed the cabin, one of the gunmen could kill Holly before they got to her. On the other hand, if they were allowed to leave, Holly would surely die. There was only one thing to do.

"Let's roll," Cole said.

The words were hardly out of his mouth before Bruce gave the command, and Cole said another prayer for Holly's safety as the SWAT team converged on the cabin.

FIFTEEN

The sound of gunshots from outside the cabin sent Holly's captors scurrying for cover. Willie and the man who'd helped him abduct them pulled guns and prepared to fire. She dropped to the floor and covered her head with her arms.

A voice from outside called out for her abductors to give themselves up, and peace flowed through her shaking body. She'd know that voice anywhere—Cole. He had come for her. She had no idea how he had found her, but she was so glad he had. And he was right outside.

Suddenly, as if it had been planned to occur at the same time, the back door and the front door both flew open. She looked up to see men in body armor with the word *SWAT* across their chests rushing into the room.

"Put your guns down!" one of the men yelled.

Willie's henchman dropped his immediately and raised his hands. Julie let out a startled scream and stared in disbelief at the guns trained on the room. Willie, however, stood there glaring at the officers, then slowly bent over as if he was going to lay the gun down. But he didn't. Instead, he pressed it to Holly's head and jerked her to her feet.

The SWAT members took another step toward him, and Willie pressed the gun harder against her temple. "It doesn't matter to me whether I kill her or not. I've got nothing to lose. So if you want this woman to live, you'll let us walk out of here and get on that helicopter."

"You're not taking her anywhere." Holly looked toward the front door to see Cole standing there, his gun pointed at Willie.

"Do you think you can stop me?" Willie sneered. "Your little girlfriend is my ticket out of here, and we're leaving right now. Get out of the way, or I'll shoot you and her both."

Cole's eyes flashed, and she knew he wasn't about to give up. He was prepared to die if it meant saving her, and she couldn't let him do that. "Where are Emma and Ethan?" she asked.

"They're safe," Cole answered. "We have them."

Holly sighed in relief. "That's all that matters, then. Move out of the way, and let us leave. I'll go with them if it means nobody else here dies today."

He tightened his grip on his gun. "I can't let you do that, Holly."

"Yes, you can. Just step aside. I don't want you to get hurt."

"Holly…" he began.

Before he could finish, she glanced up at Willie. "Let's go."

A mocking smile pulled at his lips. He glanced at Julie. "Okay. Let's go."

As he turned to speak, Holly felt the gun pull

away from her head a few inches and his arm around her waist loosen. Taking a deep breath, she threw her hands up and sank her fingernails into whatever they could reach. Willie screamed out in pain and released her completely, his hands flying up to protect his face. Seizing the opening, she twisted around and kneed him in the groin.

He staggered backward, his gun aimed at her. "You'll pay for that!"

Before he could fire, a bullet whizzed past her, and Willie fell to the floor. The SWAT team members zeroed their guns in on Julie and Willie's henchman, who raised their hands in defeat. Holly's legs weakened, and she felt herself sinking toward the floor.

Before she could, Cole's two strong arms caught her and pulled her against him. She'd held back the tears ever since she'd been taken, but she couldn't any longer. She turned her face into his chest and sobbed hysterically.

She saw the officers around her taking Julie and the other gunman out in handcuffs, but she couldn't look up at them. She heard another officer calling for ambulances, but she only snuggled closer to Cole.

After a few minutes, her sobs began to subside, and she pulled back to stare up at him. "I can't believe you found us."

He looked down at her with love in his eyes. "I'll always find you, Holly. You're a part of me, and I don't want to ever lose you."

At that moment, two officers walked in the door. One held Ethan, and the other had Emma. When they saw Holly, they began to cry and reach for her. Holly pushed to her feet and grabbed Ethan while

Cole took Emma. After she had finished showering Ethan with kisses, she exchanged babies with Cole and did the same thing with Emma.

"I think we should get them home," Cole said, and she nodded.

They stepped outside, and Holly realized night had fallen. It had only been a few hours ago that they were playing in the park, but it seemed like a lifetime had passed. Although she'd never given up hope that they'd survive their ordeal, at times it had proved to be trying.

She looked up at the sky and stared at the stars, then let her gaze drift over Cole and her two babies. The three people that she loved the most, and they were all here together tonight. *Thank You, God,* she prayed, *for keeping us safe and bringing us all back together.*

Two hours later, Holly relaxed in the den of her house and thought back over all that had happened today. Mandy and Mrs. Green had hovered over all three of them since Cole brought them home, but now the house seemed quiet. The babies had been fed and were asleep in their own beds. Although they'd endured an exhausting day, Emma and Ethan didn't appear to have suffered any ill effects from it.

She wasn't so sure about herself, however. She doubted if she would ever get over the fear she'd felt when she thought Ethan and Emma were about to be taken away from her. Eventually, she was going to have to make herself stop being so overly protective of them. She had already been upstairs three times since they went to sleep, checking on them. Maybe in time she would relax some.

She glanced at her watch and wondered what was keeping Cole. He'd left shortly after bringing them home and gone back to his office. He wanted to be there to question and book Julie, the helicopter pilot and Willie's sidekick. Then he said he would go by the hospital. She'd wanted to go with him to visit Todd, Ray, Dan and Stephen, but a call to the doctor had informed her that all four were doing well and she could visit tomorrow.

Although Willie and Richmond, along with the men they'd hired, had been shot, none of them had died and they were all receiving treatment. She hoped they lived, so they could answer to the charges that were waiting to descend on them. When it came time for their trials, she intended to be in the courtroom every day.

Tonight, she had two of the other security team members on duty, but she felt it might no longer be necessary. The danger had passed, but Cole had insisted they stay. He'd warned her that you never could tell what some fan might do after learning of her ordeal. He didn't think she'd like to have a stranger suddenly appear at her house. She had to admit she agreed with him.

She was jerked from her thoughts by the opening and closing of the front door. Cole walked into the room, and his eyes locked on her. He looked tired, but the smile on his face told her that he was glad to be back. She stood and waited for him to reach her. When he did, he let his gaze drift over her face. His Adam's apple bobbed as he swallowed, and she saw a sheen of moisture in his eyes.

He reached up and let his thumb rub across her

lips. "I was afraid I might never see you again." The words were laced with fear and dread.

"I felt the same about you," she said. "And yet somehow I knew you'd find us, and you did. How did you do that?"

He sighed, took her hands in his and pulled her down to the sofa. "It's a long story."

For the next few minutes he told her everything that had happened to him today from the time he received Teresa Wilson's autopsy report until he'd visited the hospital—just before coming back to her house—to see how all the wounded were doing. "Dan is doing great, and I talked with Todd and Ray. They all said they'd be back to work soon, and Stephen said he hoped you could finish the interview sometime."

She laughed and nodded. "My manager is already taking care of that. The network wanted to reschedule, so they could include all the facts about how we were abducted trying to do the interview. I'm sure they're wanting to garner some high ratings with the story."

"I don't care about their ratings," Cole said. "I'm just glad you're all back safely."

"Me, too."

He still held her hands, and he looked down at them as he rubbed his thumb over her knuckles. "When I was telling you about what happened today, I didn't mention your voice mail."

"I noticed that."

He took a deep breath. "I kept putting off listening to it, because I didn't want to hear you say goodbye. Finally, I listened, and I had just finished when I learned you and the twins had been kidnapped. After that, things got a little crazy."

Her heart had begun to pound, because she couldn't tell what he was going to say next. "Holly, you said that one word from me would make you change your mind about leaving. Did you mean it?"

"I did."

He took a deep breath. "Then I know what I want to say."

"What is it?"

He inched closer to her, put his arms around her and pulled her close so that his lips hovered over hers. *"Stay,"* he whispered. "That's my one word. What do you say?"

She looped her arms around his neck and smiled. "Okay."

Then she pulled his head down and crushed his lips against hers.

Cole had thought he'd sleep late after the exhausting roller coaster he'd had yesterday. But to his surprise, as soon as it was morning, he'd jumped up out of bed, excited about what this new day held. Something had happened last night that he thought never would. Holly had come back to him. Now there were decisions to be made, the most important one being how they were going to merge their two lifestyles into one. They needed to talk right away.

After showering and eating breakfast, he drove to Holly's house. When he pulled up, he didn't see any of the security team but thought they must be inside. Whistling with happiness, he bounded up the steps to the porch and pounded on the door.

The door opened, and Holly stood there, a smile on her face. "What are you doing knocking?"

He glanced around again for one of the security team. "I'm used to your team checking me out before they let me through the door. When I didn't see anybody outside, I thought they must all be indoors, and didn't want to come barging in."

"I gave them the day off," she said as she opened the door wider.

He stepped inside and turned to frown at her. "You gave them the day off? Don't you think that's a bit reckless?"

She shook her head. "Nothing can happen that's worse than yesterday. I just needed to feel free for a while." She turned and headed to the den with him behind. When they were settled on the sofa, she scooted closer and kissed him on the cheek. "I didn't expect you this morning. I thought you probably had a lot of work to do at the office."

"I do. We've got to get all the charges filed against Julie and her team of murderers, but I thought we needed to talk first."

"About what?"

He cleared his throat and stood up. He paced across the floor, then turned and walked back over to her. "Holly, I love you. I always have, and I always will. You say you want to stay here, but I'm afraid you'll change your mind. I don't think I could stand to see you grow to resent me because I took your life away."

She smiled and held out her hand. "Come here, Cole." He walked back and sat down beside her. "What you don't understand is that I haven't had a life for the last ten years. I gave up everything that I needed to make me happy when I walked away from you. I've had an existence, and it's been like a dream. I've given myself and my music to my fans, but my life has been empty. I know now that I want some peace, and I want it here with you and the twins."

"I want that, too, Holly. I want to marry you, and I want us to adopt the twins. I just want to make sure that's what you want."

She leaned closer. "It is."

"Then what are you going to do? How can you continue your career from Jackson Springs?"

"I've thought that through, too. After I heard Jason's band play, I started thinking about how many talented young musicians are trying to break into the business. All they need is someone to give them a helping hand. I want to be that person."

"How do you plan to do that?"

She took a deep breath. "Well, I'm committed to a tour for the next six months, and I want to honor that promise. A lot of people in different cities have already bought their tickets, and I don't want to disappoint my fans. Are you all right with that?"

"Of course. But after the tour, what then?"

"I want to settle down here and build a performance center. I'd like to showcase emerging artists and talented performers who are trying to get noticed, as well as doing guest performances myself. I'd also like to book some established artists to perform off and on. I think, with all the tourists that this area attracts, I could make a go of it."

A stunned look crossed his face. "That sounds wonderful. So you'd go on tour for the next six months, and then you'd come back and marry me?"

She shook her head and then smiled at the surprised look on his face. "Even though I'll be touring, I'll still have open dates when I can come home. I'd like for us to get married now and for you and the new nanny to be here taking care of the twins until I can be back for good. What do you think? Do you want to take on a wife and a ready-made family right now?"

A big grin covered his face, and he pulled her close. "That sounds like a plan to me. When is this wedding taking place?"

She bit down on her lip and tilted her head to one side. "I have to be in Nashville the end of next week. That gives us about five days. I think we better tie the knot right away if we're going to have any time for a honeymoon."

"I like the way you think," he said as his lips descended on hers.

Holly wrapped her arms around his neck and returned his kiss. Her heart that had once felt like stone now pulsed with a rhythm that told her God had indeed restored it with a heart of flesh that would beat for the rest of her life for this man—the only one she had ever loved.

EPILOGUE

A year later

Holly sat next to her husband in the small church they attended and smiled when he reached over and covered her hand with his. As they waited for the service to begin, her thoughts drifted back to how different life was now than when she'd first come back to Jackson Springs a year ago.

The performance center was nearing completion, and the opening celebration was planned for next month. The list of performers coming sounded like a who's who of country-music celebrities, and she was thankful for their willingness to participate. When she'd made her plans public, she'd braced herself for criticism, but instead she had received a lot of support. Many praised her for dedicating her efforts to preserving the country-music heritage.

It wasn't just the performance center itself that made her happy, though. It was being able to come home every day and find two toddlers waiting for her and a husband who loved all of them. She'd never felt so complete as she did now. Cole's love had given her a new outlook, and she would always be thankful they'd been able to reconcile their differences. Their life was one of harmony, peace and love.

Cole leaned over and whispered in her ear. "What are you thinking about?"

She smiled and squeezed his hand. "About how far we've come in the past year."

His gaze raked over her face. "And it's all been good."

"Yes, it has."

He swiveled in the seat to face her and frowned. "I can't help but wonder if we should have brought the children. I hated leaving them behind today."

She laughed and swatted at his arm. "Don't be ridiculous. They had no business being here today. Besides, Lisa, the new nanny, had a fun afternoon planned for them."

He picked her hand up and kissed it. "You're a wonderful mother to those kids."

"And you're a wonderful father."

He gazed at her. "The happiest day of my life was when we stood before that justice of the peace at the courthouse and got married. The second happiest day was when we went back there to finalize the adoption. That building has become one of my favorite places."

She laughed and then turned her head to stare at the front of the church. "I think they're ready to get started."

The whispered chattering of the congregation grew silent as the first chords of soft music swelled from the organ. A door at the side of the choir loft opened, and their pastor walked out and headed toward the pulpit. Jason Freeman, along with another young man, followed him.

When they were in place at the front of the church, a young woman holding a bouquet of flowers and dressed in a flowing blue dress walked down the aisle, stopped at the front and turned to face the entrance. Suddenly, the familiar melody of the "Bridal March" filled the air, and the congregation stood and turned to watch the bride's entrance.

Kathy Dennis, soon to be Kathy Freeman, stood at the start of the aisle, her arm draped through her father's, and stared at Jason, who waited at the front of the church. His smile grew larger as she came nearer.

Holly couldn't help but remember the night she had arranged to introduce the couple. She'd hoped they would like each other, but she hadn't expected that they would fall in love. Now their families and friends were here to see them united in marriage.

Fifteen minutes later, with the ceremony completed, the happy couple rushed up the aisle amid well wishes from the congregation. Holly and Cole watched them go before they stepped from their pew and filed out of the church.

"The reception doesn't start for another hour. Do you need to do anything before we go there?" Holly asked.

"I think I'll run by the office. I have a few things I need to check on. You don't mind, do you?"

She smiled. "Of course not."

When they reached their car, Cole opened the door for her. "That was a beautiful wedding," he said. "I just hope they'll be as happy as we are."

"I do, too," she agreed. "I'm so thankful that we were able to find our way back to each other."

"I am, too. Life is mighty sweet right now. I have you and the children, and we're about to open the performance center. I'm thankful for all the blessings God has given me."

He still stood beside the open door, and she leaned closer and whispered in his ear. "God's not through blessing you yet."

His eyebrows arched. "He's not?"

"No." She rubbed her cheek against his. "You're going to be a daddy again."

He jerked back from her and stared in shock. "We're having a baby?" he gasped.

"Yes. Are you happy?"

He grabbed her and hugged her against his body. "I'm thrilled." His arms tightened around her. "A baby. We're going to have another baby."

"I'm glad you're happy. It's going to be bedlam around our house with three little ones."

He laughed. "I told you when we married I wanted to fill that house with children. I guess we are well on our way." He paused for a moment and then pulled back and gazed down at her. "I've changed my mind."

"About what?"

"I don't want to go to the office. I want to go home and spend some time with my wife and children. What do you say?"

"Like you always say, it sounds like a plan to me."

She started to climb in the car, but he stopped her and pressed his lips to hers. When he released her, he helped her into the passenger seat and stared down at her before he closed the door. "Life just keeps getting better, Holly."

Then he walked around to the driver's side and they headed home to see their children.

* * * * *

If you enjoy stories about strong heroes protecting children in danger, don't miss these books:

THE BABY ASSIGNMENT by Christy Barritt
BABY ON THE RUN by Hope White

And if you're interested in other thrill-packed romances set in the Smoky Mountains, you'll love Sandra Robbins's
SMOKY MOUNTAIN SECRETS *stories:*

IN A KILLER'S SIGHTS
STALKING SEASON
RANCH HIDEOUT
POINT BLANK

Find these and other great reads at
www.LoveInspired.com

Dear Readers,

Thank you so much for reading the story of Holly and Cole, and how their love for two children brought them back together. Just like Holly, sometimes the choices we make in life don't bring the satisfaction and joy we expected. Often, it's difficult to decide on what path to take when we have decisions to make, and we can choose the wrong one if we're not careful. That is why it is so important to keep our hearts tuned to God and seek His will in everything we do. When we do that, He will guide us in the direction we should go. I pray that you will keep your heart committed to God and follow the path He has planned for you.

Sandra Robbins

COMING NEXT MONTH FROM
Love Inspired® Suspense

Available April 3, 2018

MISSION TO PROTECT
Military K-9 Unit • by Terri Reed
When Staff Sergeant Felicity Monroe becomes the target of a killer, Westley James vows to protect her with the help of his K-9 partner. But with a ruthless murderer determined to make Felicity his next victim, can Westley keep the woman he's falling for alive?

TEXAS RANGER SHOWDOWN
Lone Star Justice • by Margaret Daley
Thrust into an investigation when a serial killer calls her radio talk show, Dr. Caitlyn Rhodes turns to childhood friend and Texas Ranger Ian Pierce. And when all signs suggest the killings are a personal vendetta against Caitlyn, the two of them must uncover the truth before someone else dies.

AMISH RESCUE
Amish Protectors • by Debby Giusti
Joachim Burkholder never expected to find an *Englischer* hiding in his buggy, but now he must rescue Sarah Miller from her abductor. As they grow closer, can he keep her safe...and convince her to stay with him and join his Amish faith?

WILDERNESS PURSUIT
Mountie Brotherhood • by Michelle Karl
When archaeologist Kara Park is attacked on her dig site, her high school sweetheart, mountie Sam Thrace, saves her life. With a criminal determined to keep a dangerous secret buried, will they survive a pursuit through the Canadian wilderness?

WITNESS IN HIDING
Secret Service Agents • by Lisa Phillips
On the run after witnessing a murder, single mom Zoe Marks must rely on Secret Service agent Jude Brauer for protection. There's a killer on their trail, and safeguarding Zoe and her little boy may be harder than Jude anticipated.

SECRET PAST
by Sharee Stover
On the heels of her mother's death, Katie Tribani learns her life is a lie—she and her mom have been in Witness Protection since she was an infant. Now, with her criminal father and brother after her, she must go into hiding with US marshal Daniel Knight.

LOOK FOR THESE AND OTHER LOVE INSPIRED BOOKS WHEREVER BOOKS ARE SOLD, INCLUDING MOST BOOKSTORES, SUPERMARKETS, DISCOUNT STORES AND DRUGSTORES.

LISCNM0318

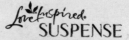

SPECIAL EXCERPT FROM

Love Inspired.
SUSPENSE

*A serial killer is on the loose on a military base—
can the Military K-9 Unit track him down?*

Read on for a sneak preview of
MISSION TO PROTECT by *Terri Reed,*
the first book in the brand-new
***MILITARY K-9 UNIT** miniseries,*
available April 2018 from Love Inspired Suspense!

Staff Sergeant Felicity Monroe jerked awake to the fading sound of her own scream echoing through her head. Sweat drenched her nightshirt. The pounding of her heart hurt in her chest, making bile rise to burn her throat. Darkness surrounded her.

Where was she? Fear locked on and wouldn't let go. Panic fluttered at the edge of her mind.

Her breathing slowed. She wiped at the wet tears on her cheeks and shook away the fear and panic.

She filled her lungs with several deep breaths and sought the clock across the room on the dresser.

The clock's red glow was blocked by the silhouette of a person looming at the end of her bed.

Someone was in her room!

Full-fledged panic jackknifed through her, jolting her system into action. She rolled to the side of the bed and landed soundlessly on the floor. With one hand, she reached for the switch on the bedside table lamp while her other hand reached for the baseball bat she kept under the bed.

Holding the bat up with her right hand, she flicked on the light. A warm glow dispelled the shadows and revealed she was alone. Or was she?

She searched the house, turning on every light. No one was there.

She frowned and worked to calm her racing pulse.

Back in her bedroom, her gaze landed on the clock. Wait a minute. It was turned to face the wall. A shiver of unease racked her body. The red numbers had been facing the bed when she'd retired last night. She was convinced of it.

And her dresser drawers were slightly open. She peeked inside. Her clothes were mussed as if someone had rummaged through them.

What was going on?

Noises outside the bedroom window startled her. It was too early for most people to be up on a Sunday morning. She pushed aside the room-darkening curtain. The first faint rays of sunlight marched over the Texas horizon with hues of gold, orange and pink.

And provided enough light for Felicity to see a parade of dogs running loose along Base Boulevard. It could only be the dogs from the K-9 training center.

Stunned, her stomach clenched. Someone had literally let the dogs out. All of them, by the looks of it.

Don't miss
MISSION TO PROTECT by Terri Reed,
available April 2018 wherever
Love Inspired® Suspense books and ebooks are sold.

www.LoveInspired.com

Looking for inspiration in tales
of hope, faith and heartfelt romance?

Check out **Love Inspired**® and
Love Inspired® **Suspense** books!

New books available every month!

CONNECT WITH US AT:

Harlequin.com/Community

 Facebook.com/HarlequinBooks

Twitter.com/HarlequinBooks

Instagram.com/HarlequinBooks

Pinterest.com/HarlequinBooks

ReaderService.com